HIS HIGHNESS THE DUKE

DRAGON LORDS: A QURILIXEN WORLD NOVEL

MICHELLE M. PILLOW

MICHELLE M. PILLOW® - MICHELLEPILLOW.COM

His Highness The Duke (Dragon Lords) © copyright 2012 - 2018 by Michelle M. Pillow

Third Print Edition July 2018

Second Print Edition April 2015

First Print Edition January 2012

Cover art © Copyright 2015

Published by The Raven Books LLC

ISBN 978-1-62501-173-2

ALL RIGHTS RESERVED.

This book or any portion thereof may not be reproduced or used in any manner whatsoever without the express written permission of the publisher except for the use of brief quotations in a book review.

This novel is a work of fiction. Any and all characters, events, and places are of the author's imagination and should not be confused with fact. Any resemblance to persons, living or dead, or events or places is merely coincidence.

Michelle M. Pillow® is a registered trademark of The Raven Books LLC

ABOUT HIS HIGHNESS THE DUKE

DRAGON LORDS 5

The would-be heroine...

Aeron wants nothing more than to live out her very long, solitary life in a small metal room listening to communications for the Federation Military. It's not glamorous. It's not even charming. But it's safe and there's no chance of getting hurt.

When she intercepts a communication about an impending attack on the Qurilixian people, she has no choice but to act. No one at the Federation seems inclined to do anything and it's up to her to save them. Desperate, she enlists the help of her degenerate sister, whose only solution is to trick Aeron into signing up as a prospective bride to the very alpha male aliens she's trying to rescue.

The man who did not need saved...

Dragon-shifter nobleman Lord Bron, is not looking forward to his seventh failed attempt at a marriage ceremony. But when he sees the lovely Aeron he knows his years of waiting have finally paid off. Fate has blessed him with a life mate...

Or have they?

His new bride is insistent she's not there for marriage, but for a mission. Dragon shifters mate for life and it's up to Bron to convince her they are fated mates, or he'll risk spending the rest of his days alone.

NEW TO DRAGON LORDS?

Dragon Lords books 1-8 follow a concurrent time line. The fun of this is that the events you read in one book might be examined from a different point of view, sometimes with overlapping or expanded scenes, sometimes with events you might have wondered about in another book. You might even discover secrets as characters interact with each other. I recommend reading them in order to get the full effect. However if you bought the books out of order, no worries, each book is technically a standalone story for the hero and heroine.

DRAGON LORDS SERIES

PART OF THE QURILIXEN WORLD
COLLECTION

Dragon Lords Books 1 - 4

The dragon-shifting princes have no problem with commitment. In one night, they will meet and choose their life mate in a simplistic ceremony involving the removing of masks and the crushing of crystals. With very few words spoken and the shortest, most bizarre courtship in history, they will bond to their women forever. And once bonded, these men don't let go...

Too bad nobody explained this to their brides.

Dragon Lords Books 5-8

The noblemen brothers aren't new to the sacred Qurilixian bridal ceremony. After several failed attempts at finding a bride, it's hard to get excited about yet another festival. No matter how honorable they try to live, it would seem fate thinks them unworthy of such happiness—that is until now.

With very few words spoken and the shortest, most bizarre courtship in history, they will bond to their women forever. And once bonded, these men don't let go...

Too bad nobody explained this to their brides.

Dragon Lords Book 9

Before four princes and four noblemen found their brides, before the death of the Var King Attor and the threat of the Tyoe miners, there was a time of peace on the planet of Qurilixen. It was not a strong peace, but it had lasted for quite some time between the cat-shifting Var kingdom and their northern neighbors the dragon-shifting Draig. It lasted because both sides had very little to do with each other.

This was the time before the great war came to rift the planet apart—dragon against cat. The only battles were skirmishes along the borderlands over territory and drunken brawls that erupted to prove which shifter side was of superior strength. It is here the dragons found their queen.

Spin-off Series

Dragon Lords is the first installment in the multiple bestselling romance series. As of this publication, there are nine Dragon Lords books.

The series continues with the *Lords of the Var®* series, Space Lords series, Dynasty Lords Series, Captured by a Dragon-Shifter series, Galaxy Alien Mail Order Brides series, and Qurilixen Lords series.

There will be more books and more series to come. They can be read alone, but the author recommends reading books in order of release.

For details please visit www.michellepillow.com

WELCOME TO QURILIXEN

QURILIXEN WORLD NOVELS

Dragon Lords Series
Barbarian Prince
Perfect Prince
Dark Prince
Warrior Prince
His Highness The Duke
The Stubborn Lord
The Reluctant Lord
The Impatient Lord
The Dragon's Queen

*Lords of the Var® * **Series**
The Savage King

The Playful Prince
The Bound Prince
The Rogue Prince
The Pirate Prince

Captured by a Dragon-Shifter Series
Determined Prince
Rebellious Prince
Stranded with the Cajun
Hunted by the Dragon
Mischievous Prince
Headstrong Prince

Space Lords Series
His Frost Maiden
His Fire Maiden
His Metal Maiden
His Earth Maiden
His Woodland Maiden

Dynasty Lords Series

Seduction of the Phoenix
Temptation of the Butterfly

To learn more about the Qurilixen World series of books and to stay up to date on the latest book list visit www.MichellePillow.com

AUTHOR UPDATES

To stay informed about when a new book in the
series installments is released, sign up for updates:

michellepillow.com/author-updates

To Lilifus the Vampire Kitty. We love you always.
We'll miss you, Lily.

1

Intergalactic Gambling Championship, Torgan Black Market

City of Madaga, Planet of Torgan

Aeron Grey tucked the full length of her long black hair beneath the black headcap, even the short bangs. The Federation Military uniform wasn't necessarily the most inconspicuous attire, but she did her best to blend in with the crowd. It was the usual ruffian mix of humanoids and other beastly creatures one would expect to see on a black market planet. Some looked like human males with only minor differences, like strange protrusions or ripples of flesh on their faces and bodies. Others were hairy, with long arms and massive chests. There were those with the skin of reptiles, large black horns, or flesh of many colors.

Some had wings. Some had webbed fingers. Every disreputable lowlife creature imaginable came to Madaga—pirates, crooked businessmen, slave traders, bounty hunters, guns for hire, and now apparently absconding Federation Military analysts looking to hitch a ride from a degenerate gambler for a long distance space trip.

"Nice costume," a humanoid man drawled as she passed nearby. He wore a feather dress and shiny red boots. "Where do I enlist?"

"I love a girl in uniform," his friend added with a high-pitched laugh. She couldn't tell if the sparkling blue skin was painted on or part of his natural alien complexion.

Aeron flinched, giving him a nervous smile as she quickly moved past. Perhaps the uniform blended more than she thought. Seconds later a swaying battalion of soldiers sauntered past in mock formation. It would appear someone hijacked a Federation Military uniform shipment and sold it at the market—which was actually pretty lucky for her.

"Come on!" One shouted excitedly, seeing her attire. "Join us!"

"Into formation, soldier!" Their leader yelled, laughing.

Aeron shook her head, backing away. She

bumped into a gurgling creature with red horns and instantly changed directions. "Excuse me."

The creature gurgled louder. Since she didn't speak Gorga, she didn't understand what he-she said.

She looked up through the glass ceiling toward the night stars. A slash of three rings split the sky into sections. They encircled the entire brown-gray planet. Aeron had flown past them while landing. From the sky, the Torganian city of Madaga was a dusty spec of hell in the shape of a desert sand dune. Up close it was a dusty gathering of adobe-style businesses built out of the brown-gray earth, shoved up against the larger complexes of metal and glass. Oh, and not only did it look like hell, it was the temperature of hell as well—at least outside on the docking platform. Inside the metal structure, the air was much cooler.

She continued navigating the crowd in the main compound, trying to focus more on the surroundings than the people. Large banners declared the much anticipated end of a year long Galactic Scavenger Hunt in a few months' time. Others flashed seductive pictures that advertised the Galaxy Playmate dancers were coming to the planet. Several of the guys in her assigned spaceport had those exact pictures stuck on their walls.

The main compound had the appearance of a

legitimate trading center, but everyone knew it was a virtual black market of fenced goods and tawdry services. If it was illegal and sought after, chances were it could be found here.

Aeron neared the round bar in the center of the room and navigated her way around the tables. This was the last place she wanted to be. The loud music, smoky atmosphere, and drunken patrons were a far cry from her well-disciplined life. She never had time for dancing and music. She rarely drank, except on leave—which, ironically, was spent alone in her room on Federation property. As she neared the far side of the bar, she hesitated. Long, metal tables stretched out before her, most of them occupied.

She didn't want to be here, but she had to be. Other people might not understand. The military wouldn't understand, or care, but she had to do this. For five months, ever since she'd heard that damned transmission about a possible genocide attack over some ore mines in the Y quadrant, she could think of little else. The planet was called Qurilixen. The Federation has no authority there, and quite frankly little interest in it but for their mining operations. The people kept to themselves and by all reports lived quite primitively. She'd reported the incident and then made a nuisance of herself until she got an answer. Unfortunately, she

HIS HIGHNESS THE DUKE

was told the Federation refused to get involved. So long as they got the ore mined on the planet one way or another, they were keeping their hands free of the whole situation. But, Aeron couldn't let it go. She couldn't stand by and do nothing. She didn't know the Qurilixen people, aside from a few facts she'd managed to dig up in the Federation archives. Regardless, to her thinking, there was only one decision to be made. She had knowledge that could save a race of people, so she was morally obligated to try.

As a civilian contracted as a Federation analyst, she was supposed to listen, translate and analyze the threat according to certain protocols. To her, genocide was the ultimate threat. A primitive people might not have the technology to get advance warning of an attack or take over. Genocide. Enslavement. Whatever the Tyoe eventually planned for the Qurilixen people, it wasn't good.

Following several sets of eyes upward, she frowned. A woman's larger than life face shone in oversized holographic contemplation. Auburn hair was slicked back to reveal a slender face.

Under her breath, Aeron muttered, "Riona. There you are. Figures you would be at the center of this crowd."

"You want a good seat, darling? Come over here and I'll let you bounce on my lap. It'll only hurt for a second. Then it'll feel real nice." The man was so hairy she could barely make out features. Large flying insects buzzed around his greasy head. He reached for her hips to make good his threat. She jumped out of his way and hurried toward Riona.

Aeron heard a woman's boisterous laughter before she found Riona at a center table in the spotlight. Metal discs floated before her in a large game grid. Tiny snaps of electricity shot between them. Fingernails tapped an inert disc as the woman contemplated her next move.

Not wanting to waste time, Aeron reached for Riona's arm and said, "Ri."

At that same moment, Riona chose to toss her disc. Her smile fell and she blinked heavily at the sudden distraction. It was too late. Her finger slipped and the disc slid off its original course, right into a strip of electricity. The unit blinked once and then fizzled as it was destroyed. Metal particles fell to the table. Chaos erupted in a series of cheers and pounding fists of protest.

Slowly, Riona stood, her returning smile strained but there. Lights flashed around them and Aeron ducked her head down to avoid the photographs. She knew the military could trace her, but hopefully one missing low-level analyst wouldn't cause too many problems or red alerts.

When this self-given mission was over, she would explain her actions and throw herself on the mercy of her Federation superiors.

Eyeing Aeron, Riona said through tight lips, "Greetings, sister. I didn't know the Federation was sending security guards to the event. You should have sent a transmission warning me. I would have told you this wasn't your scene."

Aeron stiffened at the familiar way her sister spoke to her. It was an automatic reaction. She spent most of the time denying she had any family to speak of. There was a reason for it. Her sister was a degenerate gambler who didn't take a thing seriously. If not for the big glaring hint in the form of a gambling tournament, Aeron wouldn't have been able to track her down so fast. There were hundreds of planets Riona frequented. "I need to talk to you."

"So serious. Careful, it will wrinkle your face." Riona glanced at her lost game. "Your timing is as impeccable as always."

Aeron followed her sister's unconcerned gaze to the game, not caring for the typical Riona sarcasm. "This is bigger than playtime. It's serious."

Riona glanced around the room before again looking to the game, and sighed, "I can see that."

"Would you forget about that stupid game? I need you to come with me. This is important,"

Aeron insisted. Why couldn't her sister just listen to her for once? She needed help, the kind of help only a degenerate star-traveling gambler like Riona could give. Riona knew the underbelly of the universes. She knew how to get things done. Aeron worked on a spaceport in a small metal office. Desperately, she reasoned, "When was the last time I actually came to you for help? You know I wouldn't be here if I had any other choice."

"Where are the other militants?" Riona's expression gave nothing away. She glanced around the room.

"I'm alone."

Riona studied her, surprised. "You're here on leave? You left the floating base to actually take a trip?"

"Yes, or I was on leave until… Well, no, not exactly, but once I explain you'll realize I didn't have a choice. This is about—"

Riona lifted her hand and nodded, turning serious. "Is this favor off planet?"

"Yes, but it—"

"Do you have a ship?" Riona broke in.

"Yes."

With a last glance around the crowded room, Riona said, "Then lead the way. You are family after all. Who am I to disappoint family?"

Aeron wondered at the easy agreement, but

didn't stop to question her luck. A sense of urgency filled her each time she thought of the Qurilixen. "I have a ship that can get us off planet, but—"

"Yeah, yeah, tell me all about it in flight, sis," she said easily. "We'll have plenty of time to catch up in space."

Aeron bit back a scream as her body slammed hard into the right side of the cockpit. Riona flew like she had never taken a lesson in her life. Just as Aeron was about to insist upon taking over the controls, Riona jerked the ship in the opposite direction. Aeron skidded across the floor to smack into the other side.

"Try to hold on there, sis!" Riona said, grinning.

Blast it! Her sister was enjoying this.

Riona straightened the flight path and engaged hyper drive. Aeron moaned and pushed herself up. She grabbed the back of a chair to steady herself in case her sister decided to slam on the controls again. Lights began to blur on the viewing screen and the ride became smoother. The view of Torgan's surface faded from the ship's sensors.

"I can't believe you, Ri," Aeron hissed. "I'm with you for two seconds and we're already being chased off a planet because you owe money to a space pirate. I knew coming to you was a mistake." She half expected someone to blast the ship. If not for her ordering a biological quarantine of the Torgan space docks under the guise of Federation authority, Riona's pirate pursuers would probably be giving chase. As it stood, the space pirate would have a hard time getting clearance for takeoff.

Riona pretended not to hear her, as she pushed several buttons on the console. "Ok, you got me out here. We're in space. What's so important you had to slum it with the lowlifes?"

Aeron frowned as her sister turned away from the control panel to let the ship guide itself. "I need your help. I have to get to a planet on the outer edge of the Y quadrant. I can't keep this ship."

Riona arched a brow. Aeron hated that smug look.

"The planet is called Qurilixen," Aeron explained. "The Federation has no authority there, and quite frankly little interest in it or the people, but for their mining operations. The Draig and Var people who inhabit the planet keep to themselves and by all reports live quite primitively. About five months ago, I intercepted some data that leads me to believe the people there might be in trouble. The Federation refused to get involved. So long as they get the ore mined on the planet one way or

HIS HIGHNESS THE DUKE

another, they're keeping their hands clean of the whole situation. But, after seeing our home world explode, I can't stand by and watch another race of people get wiped out—especially over something like mining rights. If something happened and I did nothing—"

"So let me get this straight." Riona's self-satisfied look only intensified. "You left work without permission and you stole a Federation ship, which you now need to ditch because you're heading to a primitive planet in the Y and don't want the military tracking you. And you need my help to get you there."

"Yes." Aeron bit her lip and nodded. "Will you help me?"

A slow smile spread over Riona's lips. "Ah, little sis, I'm so proud right now I might start crying. Of course I'll help you break a bunch of Federation laws. Besides, you know me, I'm always up for a little mischief and adventure."

"Mischief and adventure?" Aeron frowned. She would hardly dismiss her self-given mission as something so trivial. "Is that what you call what just happened down there? One minute you're playing games and the next minute we're being chased out of port by space pirates? You're lucky I was able to invoke Federation privileges and get us out of there before the pirates could make chase."

"Got anything to eat in this floating bucket?" Riona stood, completely ignoring her sister's irritation. "I haven't had a decent meal since before the tournament."

"If you found yourself decent employment, you would eat at decent intervals and wouldn't have to subject yourself to… to…"

"To having fun?" Riona ducked out of the cockpit. "To living on my own terms? To… Hey, never mind, found the food simulator! You want something?"

"A different sister?" Aeron whispered irately. "One that's sane and normal and *not* a criminal."

"THIS IS YOUR BRILLIANT PLAN?" Aeron stared at her sister in disbelief. She threw the flyer she'd gotten from one of the other passengers onto Riona's bed.

Riona lifted her head and slid the printed flyer under her face and read aloud, "Wanted: Galaxy Brides Corporation seeking 46 fertile, able-bodied Earth females of early childbearing years and A5+ health status for marriage to strong, healthy Qurilixian males at their annual Breeding Festival. Possibility of royal attendance. Must be eager bedpartners, hard workers. Virginity a plus. Apply with A5 health documents, travel papers, and IQ screen to: Galaxy Brides, Phantom Level 6, X Quadrant, Earthbase 5792461." Riona lifted her eyes, glancing up from where the personal beauty droid massaged the muscles in her back. "So you found out, did you?"

All around them was every starship convenience known to humanoids—beauty droids, cosmetic enhancements, top of the line food simulators that could materialize anything they desired, an oversized bed to sleep in. Aeron paced the length of Riona's quarters and then back again. The room was filled with machines and blinking sensors that illuminated in sections as her presence registered.

Aeron paused at an oval window full of sparkling stars. "You said you found the perfect transport. You said it wouldn't cost a single space credit. You said this ship was a relief mission to the natives of Qurilixen. You said you could get us to Qurilixen without any problems!"

"I received a free body lift this morning. I am really not seeing a problem," Riona answered. She seemed more bored than concerned.

Aeron frowned. "You didn't need a body lift."

"It was free." She arched a brow, looking like it was the most reasonable excuse in the world. "Plus free food, free massages, free beauty droid services…"

Lowering her voice, Aeron glanced at the beauty droid and stepped closer. "Galaxy Brides? Your solution was to sign up to be bartered brides? What happens when we get there? They are expecting you to get married. You can't possibly be serious about binding yourself to a stranger."

"Actually," Riona said louder, not worried about the robot servant. It did as it was programmed and nothing else. She pushed up to sit on the edge of her bed. "This is the perfect transport. It is a free ride and a pretty happy-happy one at that. Besides, I would argue that primitive males in need of brides, or else their entire race will die off, is a relief mission of sorts. Isn't that what you're trying to prevent? An entire race of people dying off?"

"Don't be dramatic," Aeron said.

"Who's being dramatic? Go check out the planetary uploads the ship provides." Riona closed her eyes and concentrated, clearly trying to assess new information she'd recently uploaded into her brain. With any upload, it took awhile for all the facts to commit themselves to memory. "Qurilixian women are rare due to the planet's blue radiation. Over the generations it has altered the men's genetics to

HIS HIGHNESS THE DUKE

produce only strong, large male, warrior heirs. Maybe one in a thousand babies turn out to be a girl." Riona opened her eyes. "Poor lugs." Then closing them again, she continued, "The fact that they have no women of their own was why the services of corporations like Galaxy Brides are so invaluable. In return, the Qurilixian people mine valuable metal that is only found in their caves. The metal is a great power source for long-voyaging starships, all but useless to the Qurilixian people who prefer living as simply as possible, as they are not known space explorers." Riona took a deep breath and gave an obnoxiously smug smile. "But you know all about the mine thing, don't you, Federation."

"Don't call me Federation," Aeron grimaced. "I thought you'd at least grown up a little in the last five years."

"Grow out of irritating you?" Riona laughed dismissingly. Then, pretending to study her newly manicured fingernails, she said, "Besides, dear sister, they are expecting *us* to get married. I had to forge your signature to get you on the ship. Really, I should think you would be grateful."

"Grateful? You are truly delusional if you think—"

"Yes, grateful!" Riona scowled. "You show up out of nowhere, ruining my victory—"

"You got us chased off Torgan by pirate loan sharks—" Aeron tried to interrupt.

"That's because you made me lose my bet. You couldn't have waited, oh, say two seconds until after my throw?"

"You almost crashed into the ceiling of the docking platform with your reckless flying."

"Blast it, Aeron, I would have been set for life! I'm lucky all that space pirate did was chase me off the planet. If you would have just waited a few seconds, I would have won fifty-thousand space credits off a side bet. Instead, I owe fifty thousand. I should have thrown you into a black hole or better yet, given you to the pirates to cover part of the debt. Then I wouldn't have had to save your ungrateful ass from them! And I didn't hit the ceiling. Give me some credit. I know how to fly a ship —better than you, I might add. I didn't ask you to come to Torgan. You did that on your own. You came to me. You ruined my life and in return I'm doing you a favor." Riona glared at her sister. "So if you're keeping score—"

"I'm trying to save a planet." This was why they didn't talk. Every conversation seemed to explode into a fight. Aeron tried to be the reasonable one. "I'm sorry if I think saving a world is slightly more important than your game."

"It's my livelihood, not just a game." Riona

HIS HIGHNESS THE DUKE

pushed a robotic hand that tried to reach for her hair, batting it away. "You always do that. You belittle what I do."

"You play games, Ri. Don't pretend that is an actual career."

"It is a career. It's my career. It's not like there is a big list of options for someone like me. Would you rather I take off my clothes with the Galaxy Playmates? Would that be a respectable enough paycheck for you?"

"You are being dramatic."

"You are being a colossal spacebitc—"

"I will not let what happened to our home world happen to the people of Qurilixen. They're primitive and cannot protect themselves from a highly advanced race of aliens." Aeron had already told her sister pretty much everything but felt the need to reiterate. "As long as the Federation gets what they want, they don't care what happens. I can't stand by and do nothing. If something happened and I did not do everything in my power to stop it… Ri, they need help. Just like our people did."

Riona's expression hardened. "Don't talk about our people. It's bad luck to speak of the dead."

"I honor them by remembering them," Aeron countered.

"Why would I want to remember a giant mine-field of floating rock?"

"Our home world was beautiful," Aeron defended.

"Until it exploded into a billion pieces," Riona yelled. "It's nothing but a black empty space now. Even the meteors have floated away."

"This isn't just about our childhood home. This is about a planet that needs saving. If the Tyoe succeed in their plans, they will kill everyone over mining rights. I can't let the Qurilixian people become exterminated when I can try to stop it."

"Send them a communication," Riona muttered.

"I couldn't. You know very well that in my position the Federation monitors all of my communications and, regardless, the Draig are not part of the Federation alliance. It's not like I can get the local nobility to take my transmission. As much as I'd like to be able to just type them a letter telling them to be careful, that wasn't an option." Aeron frowned. "Sorry you were so inconvenienced."

"Oh, that sounded sincere." Sarcasm dripped from Riona's tone.

Aeron didn't answer.

"You act like I'm heartless. I'm here, aren't I? You wanted my help and I helped you. You wanted a ride and I found you a ride. It's not like trips to

HIS HIGHNESS THE DUKE

the outer Y quadrant are around every corner, let alone trips to an isolated planet. A planet, by the way, that houses two warring classes of people, which necessitate landing on the right side of the planet. That's a pretty tall order, sis. Would you rather I hijacked a ship? Broke a few more laws you're so keen on observing?"

Aeron opened her mouth, but didn't get a chance to answer.

"Listen, we go, we smile, we pretend to consider our options, we drink, we dance or whatever it is these Draigs do for fun, and then you do what you have to and we leave." Riona began walking aggressively toward her as she continued, "Now, we have a long flight so I suggest you take advantage of all the services. Go upload mundane planetary and Qurilixen species facts into that brain of yours. Or better yet, *relax*, if you even know what that is. Have permanent polish applied to your nails. Get your breasts enhanced and enlarged so the other militants will have a reason to promote you to head analyst. Get that boulder removed from your tight ass. I don't care what it is…" She ran her hand over a wall sensor. The door to the hallway slid open. "So long as it's not in here. Have a good flight, sis, see you when we land."

Riona gave her a light push, forcing Aeron into the hall before shutting the door in her face.

Shaking with the kind of rage only her sister could produce, Aeron marched down the metal corridor to her assigned room. Under her breath, she muttered, "I hope one of the barbarians takes you home with him as a wife, and I hope they are the foulest, ugliest creatures to have ever lived!"

BREEDING FESTIVAL GROUNDS, Outside the Draig Palace, Planet of Qurilixen

Lord Bronislaw, High Duke of Draig, eyed the festival grounds before him. Servants busily worked to make sure everything was in order before the shipment of Galaxy Brides arrived. Bron wasn't necessarily looking forward to the event, being as it was his seventh year in a row, but he was duty bound to attend—especially this year, as it was the first year his four royal cousins, the Princes of Draig, would be searching for their wives. For that he was grateful. The royal family was the only family on the planet who outranked his, and the people's attention had predictably shifted from his marital pursuits to the princes'. In fact, it was almost as if the people had forgotten he was attending. As an honorable nobleman, his repeated failures were not a kind reminder to others hoping to find a bride someday.

HIS HIGHNESS THE DUKE

Bron wished he could forget he was attending. This night weighed heavily on the back of his mind all year round. Would this be the year the gods blessed him? Or would this be another failed attempt? Would he go home empty-handed to the disappointed stares and mutterings of his subjects? Looking up at the green-tinted sky, he could already see the telltale darkening of the normally light heavens. Night only came to the planet of Qurilixen once a year. It is part of what made the Breeding Festival so sacred to his people. It was the only time couples could marry.

Normally, a soft green haze of light plagued the planet's sunny surface. Qurilixen had three suns— two yellow and one blue—and one moon, which made for a particularly bright planet. To the left of the valley a colossal forest stretched into the distance. The green leaves of the foliage were over-large due to the excessive heat and moisture they received. The trees towered high above the planet's surface, thicker than some of the smaller homes in the nearby village.

"Here we go again," his brother, Alek, said as he reined his ceffyl beside Bron's. He automatically gripped the center horn of the beast to keep his balance on the wide back as it shifted. The animal had a fanged mouth that opened with a hiss of its long tongue. It had the eyes of a reptile, the face

MICHELLE M. PILLOW

and hooves of a beast of burden, and the body of a small elephant. Like all ceffyls in their stable, it was a fine steed.

This was to be Alek's fifth attempt and he looked forward to it with all the excitement exhibited by Bron. The second youngest, Mirek, faced his fourth festival. The youngest of them, Vladan, came for his first. Bron pitied Vladan for the disappointment the night would bring. He could remember his own first ceremony as if it had been the night before. He had stood with the bachelors and waited, his heart full of hope and his stomach in his throat as he searched the faces of the eligible women for the one that would be his. Only, the sacred crystal about his neck never glowed to signify he had found his true mate, his wife. He had tried to warn his youngest brother against such hope, as did the others. Vladan still carried that spark in his eyes as he looked down at the valley of pyramid-shaped tents decorated by waving banners.

As Mirek and Vladan reined their mounts next to them on the hill overlooking the festival grounds, Vladan said, "Does it always look like this?"

Bron frowned. Vladan had not heeded their example. Though he tried to hide his emotions, the youngest brother still believed this night might prove lucky.

HIS HIGHNESS THE DUKE

"Yes," Alek said. "Though they still must set up a banquet tent for potential brides and fire pits around the campsite. From this position it will look as if the entire valley is on fire." At Vladan's questioning look, he added, "We camp here after the festivities. If you do not find a bride, you do not go to the tents. Whichever tents are empty are taken down early in the morning by servants. No one wants to see a reminder of the failed attempts."

"So we will gather here tonight after the ceremony," Bron stated. He really didn't expect to take home a bride, and if they camped on the cliff they could make a faster departure in the morning. He had matters to attend to at his castle home.

"Sounds good. I have mares that are about to drop," Alek answered. As Top Breeder on the planet, it was Alek's duty to see to the ceffyl stock. They had a gestation period of three years but only made it to term about half the time. Overseeing the birthing process was very important.

"We should greet our cousins and tell the king we have arrived," Mirek said. He was the first to move.

"Yes, let's get our little brother fitted for his loincloth," Alek teased. "We wouldn't want it falling off during the festivities."

"You're right," Vladan boasted, puffing out his chest. "It wouldn't do for all the women to want me after such a display of prowess. I am only allowed one wife."

Bron gave a light brotherly snort of disbelief as he urged his mount down the hillside. "Come. Let us report to our uncle. He will want a royal accounting before all is lost to drinking and dancing."

2

Dusk claimed the small planet of Qurilixen, turning the reddish-brown earth into a dark and brilliant red. The oversized leaves drooped on their branches, as if sleeping off the long year. They emitted a subtle smell unique to the night hours. Bron's nose caught the scent easily behind the smoke of bonfires. He loved that smell.

The grooms stood in two lines, forming two walls of flesh the procession of brides would walk through to find their matches. Behind them the married men sat in throne-like chairs with their wives firmly upon their laps. Music and laughter resounded over the grounds. Bonfires cast the attendants in stark relief. Torches lit dim earthen pathways leading through the large pyramid tents beyond the main clearing. Ribbons and banners

MICHELLE M. PILLOW

floated on the breeze in many brilliant colors. Bron knew where his tent would be waiting for him, though he had never been inside it.

Darkness always brought with it a mystical feeling. It was a time when the dragon inside them lifted its head and urged the human part to play. Later, as those lucky enough to find a wife disappeared into tents, the population would spread out over the valley to engage in various pleasures.

Bron shifted his hips. As was tradition he wore a loincloth, a gold band around his bicep, a black leather mask to hide his face from forehead to upper lip, and the sacred crystal around his neck. Though they teased each other about it, his people were hardly ashamed of the naked form.

Bron had sworn to himself that he would merely go through the motions. He would not get excited, would not get his hopes up. Then the door to the Galaxy Brides' ship opened over the docking plank, and he couldn't stop his heart from quickening or his lungs from filling with air to hold a deep breath. For a long moment, silence pervaded inside of him. The world stilled.

Then chaos.

The married women burst into laughter. From his place in line, Bron saw several of the younger men shouting and posing for the prospective brides. They were too young to participate in the ceremonies, but that didn't stop them from secretly hoping one of the brides would see them and choose. It happened, rarely, but it did. Unlike the grooms, the onlookers wore the traditional tunic-style clothing of his people.

The brides waited at the mouth of the ship, appearing in a single file line that disappeared into the depths of the metal corridor. He narrowed his eyes, letting his vision shift with gold as he tried to see more details. The women were covered in the fine gauze and silk of the traditional Qurilixian gowns. The slinky material stirred against the skin when they moved, hugging tight over the hips and flaring out around the legs in thin strips. Soft silk shoes encased their feet. The gowns fell low over the breasts to reveal a generous amount of cleavage. A belt of sorts went across their backs. But, instead of looping in the front, they continued to the sides, holding the wrists low like silken chains, and winding halfway up the arm to lock over the elbows. The women couldn't lift their arms over their heads.

His blood felt as if it boiled in his veins. The women looked so soft and feminine. He ached to touch one. Closing his eyes, he tried to beg the gods for their blessing, but the words never formed. Instead, he asked them with his feelings, the yearning inside his chest that didn't need words.

Let this be the year. He'd made his offering. He lived a good life.

"I would rather face battle," Mirek whispered next to him. "This anticipation is torture."

"I cannot believe our little brother does not have to stand in even one of these greeting lines. It is almost laughable that Vladan found his wife before his first ceremony started and here we are, again." Bron was happy for his little brother, though he would be a fool to deny he was jealous—even as he was a little concerned by the match. Before the ceremony, the king had ordered they be presented to a marriageable daughter of a friend of one of the mining dignitaries. Apparently Lady Clara of the Redding was above attending their "primitive" festival and refused to marry beneath her station. She barely even acknowledged them as she coldly looked over the highest ranking nobles the Draig had to offer. In fact, when Vladan's crystal began to glow, she merely nodded, turned her back on them and left for her private dressing chamber.

"Aye," Mirek answered, chuckling. "I do not envy him that bride. I only hope that was paint on her body and not her true flesh. She will scare the children and deliver them into nightmares."

"I did not see the paint. I was too busy staring at her head. Do you think that tower of hair hides

HIS HIGHNESS THE DUKE

a skull beneath it?" Bron wasn't sure which was worse—no bride, or one whose humanoid heritage was questionable.

"Our nephews will be born with skulls the shape of pyramids." Mirek laughed. Bron knew Mirek was joking and would not be concerned by the woman's appearance. As the Mining Ambassador, he spent the most time off planet amongst alien species.

"The gods would not be so cruel," Bron answered. Even as he said it, he turned his attention to where his brother Alek waited. Alek's hand was clenched over his chest, holding his crystal as if it would crush the stone before it had a chance to work. Bron didn't approve of the gesture, but he understood the desire to be done with it all. Alek's expression was hard and his features flushed as if he'd recently shifted to dragon form and had been running through the forest. Perhaps that's exactly what his brother had done. Alek had been late getting to the receiving line. It was possible Vladan's unexplainable good luck had stirred Alek's jealousy. Better to run off his frustrations than to show them before the brides. Alek, seeing his attention, nodded once. Bron returned the gesture.

Mirek's smile faded as he, too, looked at Alek. "Would they not?"

Bron turned his attention from his brothers to

the brides. Like the previous years, Galaxy Brides did not disappoint. The women were lovely. Bron sighed, looking down at his bare feet. Firelight illuminated his flesh. The first woman walked by, drawing his attention back up. He tried not to look at them directly. It was almost over.

AERON REALLY HATED HER SISTER. If there had been any doubt before, this moment decided it. When she pictured flying in to save the primitive race of helpless miners, this is not what she had expected to find, and this was definitely not what she had expected to be wearing.

As she stepped off the docking plank onto the hard earth, she could feel the ground's texture through her thin silk slippers. She longed for her military-issue boots. A breeze stirred her gown, lifting it above her knees. She missed the comfortable familiarity of her uniform. In a gown, she felt too exposed to the elements, especially on the naked flesh of her thighs.

Inside she trembled with fear. This was why she was an analyst and not a soldier. Aeron wasn't built for adventure. She liked safety and routine and the ordinary. There was nothing ordinary about a planet filled with desperate males. What if they were sexually depraved from the lack of women? What if they tried to drag them off into… She glanced around, her heart starting to beat faster in panic. What if they tried to drag them off into the nearby tents? What if…?

Aeron forced her gaze upward, past the shoulder of the woman walking in front of her. The potential husbands were lined up in two rows, creating a path the women were to walk through— a path lined with naked male flesh. And not just male flesh, really handsome male flesh, bronzed solid muscles, piercingly lustful eyes, barely contained warrior energy. This was not safe or routine. These men represented chaos and danger. They represented everything she tried so hard to cut from her neat little life. Which meant Riona probably loved it.

Her breathing deepened in fear. What was she doing here? These men clearly didn't need her help defending themselves. How arrogant of her to think the barbarians needed her help! Perhaps her Federation superiors had been right. This was none of her business. Her feet stopped moving for a brief moment as she thought of turning back around. It was useless. A woman bumped into her back and gave a soft swear of protest, forcing Aeron forward.

Fur loincloths clung to masculine hips. Golden bands of intricate design clasped around sinewy biceps. From their solid necks hung crystals bound with leather straps. Aeron tried not to stare, but it was a little hard. Firelight glistened on their oiled bodies. The Qurilixian males were every inch the proud warrior class they were rumored to be, some even seemed to tower nearly seven feet tall.

Some of the crystals around the men's necks began to glow, signifying they'd met their mates. Agreements were made already? How? Nothing was said. Had she missed some piece of vital information on the ship? She tried to close her eyes to access the uploaded information, but the woman behind her shoved her forward none too gently.

Galaxy Brides had provided them with uploads of the planet's culture. It was on the outer edge of the Y quadrant, inhabited by primitive males similar to Viking clans of Medieval Earth. The Qurilixian worshipped many gods, favored natural comforts to modern technical conveniences, and actually preferred to cook their own food without the aid of a simulator. They were technically still classified as a warrior class, though both sides were said to be peaceful for nearly a century—aside from petty territorial skirmishes that broke out every fifteen or so years between a few of the rival houses. All the cold hard facts uploaded into her brain did not prepare her for the reality.

Aeron pulled her arms close to her body as she

HIS HIGHNESS THE DUKE

neared the first male. The grooms looked as if they might reach out and grab hold at any moment. The fear inside her grew. She wanted to run. But where? Behind the statuesque bridegrooms were a rowdy bunch of men posing for their attention. The unruly men were dressed in tunics and pants, but the large barbaric size of them was evident. At least the grooms weren't moving, not like the surrounding crowd. She hugged her arms tighter.

"I hate you, Ri. I hate you. I hate you," she whispered, as if the words could somehow give her strength. They didn't. Even as she said it, she knew her current situation was mostly her own fault. "I hate—I have a mission. I have a mission. I ha…"

Her words trailed off as her attention was pulled sharply to the side. Electricity shocked the full length of her body, but the strange thing was nothing touched her to account for the sensation. One of the tall warriors caught her attention and held it. His head was down as he looked at his feet. Dark brown shoulder length hair hid his masked face from view. She had a peculiar urge to push that hair aside, to feel its thickness through her fingers, to lift his eyes to hers. However, his crystal was glowing with a bright inner light. A small wave of disappointment filled her. He was taken… *not* that she wanted to marry the man. There was no way a woman like her could stay in a place like this.

Her heart would surely give out from the constant fear.

Aeron quickly averted her gaze and walked faster, willing the woman in front of her to move. The memory of bronzed flesh and bowed head wouldn't leave her. The man was built like the other natives—intimidatingly thick chest, corded neck, the oh-so-defined hip and stomach muscles like some of the more advanced Federation fighters had. Modern technology could only take the human body so far. The rest was hard physical work.

Aeron kept her head down and kept walking, refusing to make eye contact with any of the locals. It was with relief that she made it to the end of the procession. The crowd had quieted, not that she'd noticed when or how. Her heart beat so loud she could hear it in her ears. A cool breeze pressed the flimsy material of her dress against her body. She felt too exposed. She couldn't look up. The short veil affixed to her upswept hair tickled her cheek. She made a move to swipe it away, but the silken belt connected to her wrists kept her hands down.

Unable to help herself, she peeked back over her shoulder. The ship stood tall in the background, the docking plank lifting. The bachelors stared after them. Not all of them had glowing crystals, but several did. Her gaze moved to the man with a

HIS HIGHNESS THE DUKE

bowed head. He no longer looked at the ground, but now stared after the brides. Aeron quickly turned before his eyes met hers. He was more handsome than she could have imagined—even with a mask hiding half his face. Too handsome, if the truth was told. Men that beautiful made her nervous. She preferred men who were... Well, if her dating record was any indication... Who in the black hole of Hades was she trying to fool? The very idea of her having a dating life was laughable.

With little choice but to follow where the other brides led, Aeron made her way to a raised platform where a gigantic feast had been laid out. Her sister was already seated with a drink in her hand by the time Aeron found her place at the table. She kept her eyes averted, hoping not to draw too much attention. To not eat would be rude, but she should be able to duck away after the meal to wait out the ceremony.

LORD BRON STARED at the glowing crystal about his neck. He'd been so lost in thought, so preoccupied with the idea of never finding his life mate, that he hadn't been paying attention to the procession of brides. How could he have missed his future wife? She was here. This was his night. And he didn't even know which one she was. To admit he hadn't been looking as she passed would be an insult not only to her, but to his pride. But then, how to find her?

His heartbeat quickened. Which one? Tradition held that he'd know the moment he looked at her, but he hadn't been looking. Desire and hope built within him. He grabbed hold of his crystal, feeling its energy pulse against his hand. Finally. A bride!

He would know her when he saw her, but for now he had to go give thanks to the gods. Turning, he walked in the opposite direction of the brides. He wanted to shout his good fortune, but instead kept quiet as was tradition. The men who had been blessed needed to go to the temple and give thanks. Those who were not fortunate needed to drown their sorrows in stout liquor.

"It is a good year," Mirek said beside him. "Many blessings on your union, brother."

Bron automatically looked down to Mirek's chest. His crystal lay dormant. Sadness filled him for his brother, and he knew whatever he said in comfort would prove futile, so he said nothing.

"I will attend to the campsite before traveling home," Mirek said. "I will not wait for you. Enjoy your good fortune."

Bron nodded once as Mirek pulled away to go with the others who had not found mates.

HIS HIGHNESS THE DUKE

Alek moved to join him, pausing to receive Mirek's words of blessing on the way. Alek's crystal glowed but there was a strange look in his eyes.

"Is all well?" Bron asked.

Alek gave a small laugh, but the effort was forced. "What could be wrong? Three of us have been blessed, as well as all of our princely cousins. For whatever reason, the gods have finally decided to smile upon us. It is a good night for all but Mirek. Let us give thanks and collect our brides before the gods realize what they have done and change their minds."

"Don't even think such things," Bron scolded, worried that his crystal would stop glowing because he didn't know the face of his woman. He glanced behind him, hoping for some jolt of recognition as he caught a glimpse of a couple of the women. Nothing came to him and he was forced to join the others at the temple.

3

Aeron wasn't hungry, but she forced herself to partake of the roasted two-horned pigs and blocks of Qurilixian blue bread with whipped cheese. The meal was laid out on large trenchers, set directly before the brides, and spread over long wooden tables. Servants carried pitchers, as if their entire purpose was to ensure that each woman's goblet stayed filled with a berry wine they called *Maiden's Last Breath*. Aeron was moderate when it came to drinking, but the sweet taste was delicious and the liquor did much to calm her shaking hands.

"I don't know why I'm so nervous," she whispered to herself for lack of anyone to talk to. "It's not like I'm about to get married."

Most of the Galaxy Brides' women dined in a strange state of excited silence, whispering and giggling. Others flirted with the handsome servants. With the straps on the gowns, it was hard for the brides to lift their arms, so the servants retrieved anything they desired for them. Some even went so far as to offer the women food by their own hands, her sister Riona being one of those brazen women.

Aeron hadn't really connected with any of the women on the ship, not like her sister. Instead of socializing, she looked over the campground. The bachelors were gone and the people she could see all looked the same. It was impossible to tell who was in control and who was merely a subject of the realm.

The married couples dined around the campfire at a distance from the prospective brides. Wives fed their husbands in a sensual display of romance. Aeron tried very hard not to stare, even as she thought it barbaric. The entire place was chaos and it made her extremely uncomfortable.

"Are you nervous?"

Aeron blinked, looking to her side at the question. She recognized Nadja from the ship, but the woman wasn't talking to her. The question had been directed at another shipmate, Morrigan. Nadja whispered something and began to laugh.

"Yes," Aeron whispered, answering the question that wasn't meant for her. "I'm very nervous. I wish I was home where it's safe and predictable."

A glance at her laughing sister showed Riona was not having the same lonesome time. It figured. Riona always made fast friends no matter where she was.

"They're very big, aren't they?" Nadja said to Morrigan.

"Yes, the men are very large," Aeron whispered again, still talking to herself as she thought of the bridegroom with the bowed head. A servant lifted a brow as he looked questioningly at her, but she waved him away. She listened for more of the conversation, but her eavesdropping proved fruitless and she finished her meal in silence.

Music lifted over the campground, growing loud enough to be noticeable. Aeron took a quick drink of the berry liquor. The low rhythm produced an almost euphoric effect on the brides. Their voices lowered and disappeared. Eyes turned down the platform to where the handsome bachelors were gathering before them. Aeron watched as the first man stepped forward to claim his bride. The woman came around the table, slipped her hand into his and allowed him to lead her away.

Not all of the men who had been in line were in the tent. Perhaps they hadn't connected with anyone and decided not to marry this year. Another man came forward, then another. Riona had a smirk on her face as she watched, clearly finding much amusement in the process. Aeron swallowed, nervously waiting for it to be over so she could make inquiries as to who was in charge to deliver her information before the Galaxy Brides ship took off.

When much of the room had cleared, a single man remained at the tables. He'd caught her attention when he first entered the area—the man with the bowed head. Now his gaze was trained fully on the women, as if studying them. His crystal necklace glowed brilliantly. A jolt of electricity ran through her and she forced her eyes away from the loin-clothed specimen. Heat filled her cheeks even as she averted her gaze. He was so big and strong and handsome and scantily clothed.

Aeron clenched her hands in her lap, waiting for him to grab his woman and go. She didn't like what his half-naked presence did to her. It had been a long time since she'd used transmitters to exchange pleasure essences with a man. She found that most males preferred the actual physical act of sex to a sensation exchange. However, 'real sex' was something Aeron could not participate in. When she did meet someone, her way of doing things turned out to be more of a novelty experience for them rather than any deep connection they had to her. Since she had a hard time letting people get

HIS HIGHNESS THE DUKE

close, those opportunities didn't present themselves often.

Her body heated as she detected the last groom to finally move. He stepped on the platform at the far end of the table and began to walk past the remaining brides. It was strange, considering the others had gone directly to their chosen mates. Had he forgotten who he'd picked? The thought caused her to laugh softly to herself. Suddenly, heat forged its way through her body, coursing through her blood. The laughter died in her throat. She held very still, not daring to look up as the man moved passed. Only, he wasn't moving. He was standing before her. Somewhere in the back of her mind, she heard Riona chuckling.

When he didn't move, she glanced to the side. His naked waist was directly in front of her. The tight muscles were so close she could reach out and touch his oiled flesh. A finely carved navel drew her attention to the rippled plains leading up the center of his chest. She stared at his stomach, not moving, not speaking, and probably not breathing though she was too dumbstruck to actually check her vital functions at the moment.

Move, her numbed brain ordered him. Her lungs began to burn and her head became dizzy. She blinked, fighting the lightheadedness swimming in her head. No, she was definitely not breathing at the moment.

Bron looked at the bowed head of the bride, waiting for her to look up at him. His eyes had found her as he'd first come to the tent, but as she wouldn't look directly at him, he couldn't be sure she was actually his. He hoped. He assumed. He wanted it to be her, but he had to be sure first. To be certain he had crossed before the remaining women, watching their faces, feeling his emotional reaction to them, studying the glow of his crystal.

And, as he stepped before the raven-haired beauty, he was convinced. He didn't need the crystal to tell him he'd found the one. Every part of him pulled toward her like a Yorkin to a baited trap of fresh meat. His stomach was tight and already he felt the torturous lift between his thighs when he looked at her. Oh, how he ached. The years of desperation propelled his desires to agonizing proportions. He doubted he would make it through the night without claiming her in a completely raw, potent, beautifully perfect physical sense. Unfortunately for him and his desires, tradition dictated he wait until after the wedding night to do the things he wanted to her. This was a night of discovery and

HIS HIGHNESS THE DUKE

acceptance, not claiming. To take her body would be to shame himself and his family's honor. As the oldest brother and the High Duke, he could not afford to tarnish his family name.

Dark hair was pulled up beneath her short veil. Her front locks were cut short against her forehead. The delicate line of her neck and shoulder was formed of soft, touchable skin. He wanted to run a finger down the length of her neck and feel the pulse he saw thumping gently against her throat. She wasn't built hard like his kind. Rather she appeared almost fragile, as if she would break when he lifted her into his arms. He made a mental note to only touch her with gentleness for fear she would actually shatter into tiny pieces.

It didn't appear that she was breathing, or that she had any intent of acknowledging him. Her head turned slightly to the side, so that he could see the angle of her jaw and corner of her mouth, but little else. Why would she not look at him?

"Move," he detected her to whisper in the old star language. The sound was very soft and low, but as a shifter he could hear such things easily. Was she angry with him for not acknowledging her earlier and now sought to slight him in the same way? He watched the steady beat of her pulse and listened to the shallow intake of her breathing. Her muscles were not tense. She didn't appear upset.

45

It occurred to Bron that perhaps this meekness was a custom of her people and so he finally made the first move. He reached to touch the smooth flesh of her cheek. The very glance of it against his fingers caused a pleasurable sensation to course through him. Wanting more, he let his fingers glide over her face to turn her attention up toward him.

Dark blue eyes found his. For a moment he just looked at her. She wasn't smiling at him. In fact, she had little expression on her face whatsoever. As much as he wanted to keep touching her, he knew he should let go before he disgraced himself all over the bridal table.

Withdrawing his hand, he said, "I am Bron, come."

Her mouth opened, then closed, opened, then closed. Finally, she nodded once. "Greetings, Broncome. I am Aeron."

Bron's mouth twitched at that. "My name is Bron."

She glanced around before looking up at him. Hesitantly, she answered, "Greetings, Bron. I am Aeron." Her words were slowed, as if she didn't expect him to understand them.

"Come, Aeron," he said. The sound of laughter caught his attention, and he glanced over to see a woman with auburn hair and light brown eyes watching in merriment. Her features carried some of the same shapes as Aeron's, but not enough that he would stake his life on their relation.

Aeron didn't move.

"Come," he repeated, holding out his hand.

Slowly she stood. Instead of walking around the table to join him, she leaned forward and whispered, "I'm sorry. I don't understand what's going on. Aren't you supposed to go find your bride? The one that made the crystal glow?"

At that he frowned. How could she not know? He glanced down at his crystal. It pulsed brightly, not that he needed the necklace to tell him what he already felt deep inside. Well aware that he was being watched, he leaned forward and whispered back, "Come. We will discuss this further in private."

Aeron glanced around, apparently coming to the same conclusion he had. She nodded once and made her way around the table. The auburn-haired woman laughed louder. The sound was punctuated by the slap of her palm on the wooden tabletop. Bron had the strangest urge to throw something in her direction, though he would never act upon such an impulse.

Before he could offer his hand, Aeron pulled her arms closely against her chest effectively cutting him off. Her steps were hurried as she led him from the banquet table, away from the onlookers. If he expected her to relax when out of the spotlight, he was mistaken. She only tensed more when they were somewhat alone.

"Come," he said, urging her to follow him to his tent.

She glanced around before nodding once. Her steps were slow, almost agonizingly so. He wanted to pick her up and cart her off, but remembered his decision to be gentle with her. Surely such rough handling would not be welcomed by one as delicate as she was.

"Where are we going?" she asked, the words low as if they were being followed.

"Come," he answered, unable to say anything else. Traditions were very clear and he did not wish to test the gods' tempers by breaking them. Already he had said too much to coax her to come with him. It had taken him seven ceremonies to find her. He would not, *could* not jeopardize his happiness now. The woman would be his only chance. If he didn't win her tonight, his life might as well be over. Without her, he would not have love, or a wife, or children. An almost desperate feeling gripped him and he tried to breathe past the pain and fear trying to invade his chest.

"Did I do something wrong? Am I in trouble? If this is about my paperwork, I can explain what happened, if you tell me what happened." The woman stopped walking. "Please, where are you taking me? I promise there is a good explanation for whatever it is I have done."

Bron placed a hand on her arm and urged her to walk beside him once more. He smiled to ease her nervousness. "Come."

AERON WASN'T sure where she was going or why. She could assume it had something to do with the paperwork her sister turned in for her. What if the Federation picked up on her name in one of their routine scans of the airwaves? What if they had someone in the area to pick her up? She glanced at the sky. There weren't any ships hovering that she could see.

Her new friend apparently wasn't going to tell her anything. Perhaps his knowledge of the star language was limited. Most Federation planet dwellers could speak it, but this wasn't a Federation planet. If the sounds coming from around the bonfires were any indication, he spoke a guttural local dialect with harder syllables and gruffly flowing words. There was an exotic charm to the sound, but she imagined the unfamiliarity of it would soon get tiresome to a non-speaker.

She hugged her arms tightly to her chest,

careful to keep an eye on the incredibly large warrior man leading her through the makeshift village of tents. The hand on her arm sent little sparks of warm awareness through her. She swallowed nervously, unsure what to do. If not for Riona's annoying laughter, she might not have even followed him this far. The man's deep gaze did something to her insides. They made her all melty and trembly. Neither sensation was bad, per se, but they definitely were not welcomed.

The path between two tents narrowed and he let go to walk slightly ahead of her. She allowed her gaze to roam over his back. It was as well defined as the front side. The loincloth brushed along the tops of his thighs, swaying ever so gently against his tight ass. Every inch of him was smooth and strong —thick arms, broad shoulders, steady legs, purposeful gait. She took a raspy breath of air, trying to calm her overactive libido.

It was only when he stopped before one of the pyramid tents and lifted the flap, that she realized he'd led her to the end of the campground. The dark colossal forest blocked the distance from view. Aside from the glow of bonfires in the night sky, she couldn't see the banquet area through the field of tents.

Not sure why, she ducked inside. The large pyramid's ground was covered with fur rugs. It

HIS HIGHNESS THE DUKE

crushed softly beneath her slippers as she stopped walking. Bron moved behind her, but she didn't look to see what he was doing. Her attention was caught by the giant bed in front of her. The massive piece of furniture stood in the middle of the tent. Silk hung from the top of the pyramid to encase the bed.

Torchlight flickered erotically along each surface. Slowly, her eyes moved to the side. In each of the three corners were three very different arrangements, each blatantly erotic and impossible to ignore. The first was a table of food and wine pitchers. It wasn't that food necessarily was erotic so much as how the food was displayed. Mounds of cream were topped with bits of fruit in what could only be compared to the female breasts. The imagery made her think of her own breasts covered in such a way, ready to be devoured. Aeron tried to cross her arms over her chest, but the belt restraint held them low.

The next corner was a steaming tub of water. An array of oils and strange bottles surrounded it. The basin was big enough to hold three people. Finally glancing at the oversized Bron, she quickly amended—two people. In the third corner a table had been set up with an array of silk straps, iron shackles, an assortment of whips and other items she'd rather not look at too closely.

51

"Decide," Bron said when her gaze turned to his. The low accented words were foreign yet seductive. The fire from the torches danced in the depths of his dark eyes. She wished she could see his face, but the mask hid his features from view.

"Decide what?" she asked, almost afraid of what the answer would be. She looked at his neck, to the bright glow of the crystal. Only then did the full realization of why he'd asked her to follow him sink in. Somehow, he thought she was his bride. She had been so worried about being caught by the Federation before she had a chance to talk to the Draig authorities, that she hadn't considered one of the men actually mistaking her for a mate.

His lips twitched up in amusement. He had a great mouth. The low sigh that followed the expression was unmistakable. The firelight in his eyes seemed to come to life, as if illuminating from within him rather than a reflection.

"I think you found the wrong woman. You see, I'm not actually here to get married. I'm here to talk to one of your superiors about something that is classified." She motioned to his neck. "You can turn that necklace off now."

His smile faded and for a long moment he didn't move, merely stood before her. He touched his glowing crystal, as if considering it. She took a slow step away from him, concerned by the overly serious way he was looking at her. If he chose to take her by force there would be no stopping him. His size against her laughable fighting defense abilities?

Yet she didn't feel aggression in him. He made no move to harm her. In fact, his movements appeared purposefully gentle, as if he kept himself back from her as not to scare her. The gesture was greatly appreciated. She couldn't fight off this man and her desire for him at the same time. Aeron breathed heavily, trying to calm her nerves. The sooner she found a way off this planet, the better.

BRON BOWED HIS HEAD, staring into the depths of his crystal. What was happening? What did she mean she was not here for marriage? She was with the brides. Galaxy Brides Corporation had assured them all the contracts were in order. As he did every year, the palace steward had read them over and confirmed the assessment. No chance would be taken when it came to the happiness of marriage.

Bron's crystal glowed brighter when he was around her. He felt its energy inside him, telling him that she was meant to be his wife, his life mate, his High Duchess. Beyond that, his body pulled toward her, every fiber inside of him needing her.

That was all the proof he needed. This woman was to be his wife. She was his destiny. That was all he needed to know. The rest were just details.

His heart began to physically ache, as if one of King Attor's evil Var soldiers reached inside his chest and squeezed. The Var were their sworn enemy, living to the south of the Draig borders. At this moment, he'd rather face a hundred of the Var cat-shifters than the disheartening words of this woman. If she refused him, he would be forever alone. This was his one chance, a chance that came after several hard years of worrying and waiting. He couldn't let her go. He needed to convince her.

Bron took a deep breath. He was a warrior. He was a man of honor. He did not back down from a challenge. He would prove himself worthy and his family line would be blessed by his marriage. No matter what it took, the delicate, nervous woman before him would be his wife.

"Decide, Aeron," he said, wishing he was allowed to say more. But, until she made her decision, he had to trust fate. He couldn't say too much, only prove himself in actions. He thought about touching her, proving to her that she felt as strongly as he did, but something in her face kept him back. It wasn't necessarily fear, but a deep apprehension. He didn't want to scare her away from him.

Patience. He needed patience.

HIS HIGHNESS THE DUKE

And an ungodly amount of luck.

Most men loved this night, joked about the teasing games, bragged good-naturedly about how they got their wives to accept them. Seven years of waiting had taken their toll on him and he was ready for the decision to be made. Bron didn't want games or wondering. Not right now. He wanted to know she was his, forever. He forced himself to calm. He had to trust the gods knew what they were doing.

"I'm not sure what you're asking me to decide, Bron," she said. Her words were slow and very pronounced. "Perhaps we could find someone who speaks the star language fluently?"

"I speak fluently," he answered.

Walking to the table where binding straps had been laid out, he scooped up several into one hand. Purposefully, he laid one at each corner of the bed. Her eyes never left him and he caught her looking him over with interest. He relaxed a little. At least she was not immune. He took a deep breath, catching her scent. Yes, definitely interested. The smell of her unfurling desire filled his head. It took every bit of training he had not to throw her down and give in to his animal instincts.

Slowly, he crawled onto the bed to lie on his back. He lifted his arms to the straps and spread his legs, offering to let her tie him up. If it would help

MICHELLE M. PILLOW

her nervousness—not to mention keep him from losing his mind and devouring her whole—he was very willing to let her bind him and explore. Well, at least let her go first. Later he would be doing the same to her, but that would have to wait until after the Breeding Festival was over. There would be no consummation this night.

"Decide," he whispered.

"Oh, you mean for us to…" Aeron looked around the tent nervously. "I'm flattered by your offer of physical sex, but unfortunately I…" Her hands lifted and were caught by the traditional gown's ties. "Excuse me a moment, it would be rude to rip the gown since technically I'm not here to marry and will need to return it to Galaxy Brides. But I really need to get out of these," she strained her arms against the straps, "these things."

There wasn't much privacy within the tent, so she went to the corner of the bed and hid behind the revealing gauze near his head. Bron silently rolled off the bed and moved to get a better view. Consciously she kept her back toward him as she slid out of the gown and leaned over to pull the straps off her arms. He watched the material glide off her flesh to reveal the delicate curve of her hips and ass. The scent of her became stronger.

Sweet. So sweet. And so fragile.

He clenched his fists, resisting temptation. Bron

HIS HIGHNESS THE DUKE

stepped into her peripheral view. She quickly pulled the gown back on, leaving the straps off her arms. Taking the now dangling material, she wrapped and tied the straps around her waist. Her mouth opened, as if intent on scolding him for watching, but he interrupted her.

"Beautiful," he said. "Decide."

Bron shifted his hips, trying to relieve the pressure of the material against his sensitive arousal. Aeron quickly looked away and politely pretended not to have noticed his reaction to her. He suppressed a laugh. There was no shame in wanting.

He wanted to touch her. The elders had warned the grooms that this night would be one of the hardest of their lives. He hadn't fully understood what they meant until this moment. The Draig kind acted on instinct, but on this night honor dictated they go against instinct, fight their innermost desires, and abstain from claiming the one thing they were meant to want most. To resist temptation was to show respect to their mate. It was to deny themselves for the comfort of the women, to prove they were able to act with reason and dignity. It was to give them the freedom to make the decision without the pressure of an overzealous husband letting things go too far. Temptation was fine, even encouraged, for the chase was enjoyed by many of his kind. Bron would gladly chase this woman across the universe, if only she would put him out of his current misery and claim him as her husband.

Aeron's eyes traced the edges of his mask. He willed her to take it off of him, to signify her acceptance of their future and to free him to speak without restrictions.

"Would you mind removing your…?"

He grinned. No, he would not mind it at all. He'd remove anything she asked him to.

"I uploaded the information Galaxy Brides had available on the ship, though some of the information conflicted what I previously heard about your planet. Logically speaking, I have serious doubts as to the accuracy of Galaxy Brides' reporting practices. Some of their claims about this planet seemed a little too much like propaganda and there was no language upload. Prospective brides should at least be able to understand the native language. I have half a mind to contact the… Sorry, I digress. I was saying, I know the mask is part of your ceremony, but could you take it off without it meaning marriage?"

He frowned, but nodded. Yes, after the ceremony he could remove the mask himself if she did not do it by morning's light. It was not as if the failed bachelors were expected to live with the

HIS HIGHNESS THE DUKE

shameful reminder of their unsuccessful wedding nights for the rest of their lives. No mask was needed in such a case. Those men who did not keep their brides wore the scars within for the rest of their lives. It could be seen in their hollow eyes and dead hearts. Such men were painful to behold.

Bron willed her to take the material from his face, aware that she may possibly have misunderstood him when he answered her with merely a nod. But, tradition deemed him to be mostly silent and technically it was not a lie, not technically. He would not end up a hollow shell of himself. No, he would marry this woman. He had to.

"Oh, good. It is unsettling to have a conversation when I can't see your face." Aeron gave a small sigh.

Bron leaned his head toward her and angled it to the side, not lifting his arms. He would *not* be one of those unfortunates who failed. Let her misunderstand. When he could speak openly, he would explain all she wanted to know. She reached for the material and pulled. A great relief washed over him. It was done. Lady Aeron was his.

4

Aeron started to relax when Bron didn't act aggressively toward her, at least not aggressive in a way that made her fear for her safety. It would appear, though barbaric in attire and primitive of planet, he was a gentleman—despite the physical invitations and non-too-subtle innuendos.

As the mask revealed its secrets, her breath caught. She hadn't been expecting his strikingly handsome face to be more intimidating than the faceless mask. His expression was probing. She thrust the mask toward his chest and let go. It slid down his tight body. Without looking, he caught the material in one hand at his waist and tossed it aside. Aeron followed it with her eyes to where it landed on the ground.

When she looked back at him, he had moved

MICHELLE M. PILLOW

closer. Aeron shivered. There was lustful intent in his gaze. His nose was straight, his cheekbones high like his people, leading to deep set eyes. She drew her fingers forward to hold him back, but then thought better of it as they neared his stomach. Heat radiated from his body, the sensation more intimate than any she'd felt in a very long time. The smell of him wafted around her—fresh breeze and earth and erotically charged male. Her back hit the corner of the bed, all too aware of his nearness.

"A wise decision," Bron said. "Now we may speak openly."

"Ah, uh, thank you?" Aeron inched to the side. His eyes followed her but he didn't stop her. When she managed to put distance between them, she took a deep breath. She had hoped to talk to him to find out who she needed to give her information to, but seeing him made the words stick in her throat. Taking the mask off was supposed to make her feel at ease. It didn't work. "I shouldn't have asked you to take off the mask. We should get back to the feast. Maybe you can put it back on and find someone else to do the ceremony with—"

"It is late. The feast tables are being cleared. If you desire food that is not here, I will summons a servant to bring more. It is the greatest desire of my people to be of service to you this night." He moved toward the table and pinched a fruit nipple from the mound of cream. Every practical thought left her. Her nipples strained against the gown, instantly becoming hard and sensitive. Bron turned, carrying the pinched fruit toward her. Thick cream ran slowly down his thumb to his wrist. Lifting it near her mouth, he let the fruit brush against her bottom lip. "I will be happy to feed you, my lady."

"That won't be necessary," she whispered, not really paying attention to her own words.

"Necessary? No. But very enjoyable."

Aeron was at a complete loss for words. She didn't even know how to begin to answer. His eyes stayed on hers as he leaned forward to her lips. His tongue darted out to lick the cream he'd rubbed against her. A low moan left him. A loud gasp escaped her. She jumped back, instantly rubbing her mouth. He grinned, making a confident show of placing the fruit between his teeth and chewing, before licking the cream off his hand.

"I understand there are not many women on your planet, but I am not here to entertain offers of physical sex," Aeron said.

"We are not allowed to be completely intimate this night, Aeron, so there is no reason for you to worry," he answered.

"Oh." Was that disappointment she was feeling? Aeron forced the feeling away. She couldn't

MICHELLE M. PILLOW

have sex. Ever. To do so would be to sign her own death sentence.

"But we can enjoy ourselves, explore," he paused, reaching for his waist. Unashamedly, he pulled at his loincloth, turning the material to the side in such a way as to bare the front of his waist and hips. His cock was full, as if volunteering to be the source of her exploration. "Touch, kiss." He quickly hooked his finger in the front of her gown and jerked her forward. The motion caused her bodice to slip off a breast. His hand replaced the material, cupping the soft globe. "I wish to pleasure you."

"We shouldn't. I can't. I'm here to talk to one of your—"

"Shh, tonight is not for such things," Bron admonished. "The only business to be discussed tonight is that of marriage."

His hands began to move over her body— sliding up her hip, molding against her breast, traveling along the fastenings of the gown to quickly do away with the impeding garment. Flesh met flesh.

"I thought we couldn't be completely intimate," she whispered.

"Would you like me to bathe you?" he asked in his irritatingly seductive accent.

"I don't do this kind of thing," she answered.

"I could feed you. Or we could lie on the bed if

HIS HIGHNESS THE DUKE

you prefer?" His hands reached around for her ass, pulling her tight against him. "If you are fearful of me, I will gladly let you tie me down and have control."

His eyes glinted with an inner fire. Aeron had seen many alien species. Well, she'd actually read about them in Federation databases more than seen them up close and personal. She wondered what that little light meant, if anything. Did his eyes see things differently than hers?

"You may explore every inch of me," he offered. "I will not stop you."

She automatically looked down. It was a mistake. The distinctive press of his male honor lifted between his thighs. He made no move to hide it. She clamped her legs together.

"Or I will be honored to explore you first," he lowered his voice to a whisper. "Please, give me permission to pleasure you. Let me put my tongue between your legs."

"I don't think we should be having this kind of conversation." Aeron took a deep breath.

"If not my tongue, then at least my hand?" The back of his hand brushed low against her stomach, tickling with the gentleness of it. She felt the cool air against her naked breasts but couldn't summons the willpower to cover them. Her nipples strained for his heat. "Let me taste you on my fingers."

His hand slid lower as a fingertip reached the top of her slit. Cream moistened her sex in anticipation. She dug her toes into the fur rug. Aeron didn't dare move.

"I don't think we should be doing this." She pushed at his chest. There was no moving him. Her hands slipped along his flesh in an unintentional caress. His breathing deepened and he let loose a long, low growl. The finger hovering near her pussy didn't move.

"Mm, shall I kiss you?"

"I don't think we're having the same conversation." Aeron knew she should put up a fight, or protest, or at least remember herself long enough to form a good argument as to why this should not be happening at all.

"Shall I massage you?"

"Ok, we really are not having the same conversation. I need you to stop so I can think." Her entire length tingled, from the top of her head, down to her aching breasts and damp sex, straight to her curling toes.

Bron sighed and let her go. His expression fell. "Very well. It will be as you wish for the moment, but I will ask you again and you will eventually give in to me."

Aeron had not expected him to stop. She stood naked before him. His eyes roamed unabashedly

HIS HIGHNESS THE DUKE

over her flesh, openly examining every inch. She quickly gathered her gown and struggled to put it on.

"Though I do enjoy undressing you, there is no need to put the gown on. I've already memorized every sweet inch of you, my lady." His grin was positively wicked. He took the finger that had been so close to giving her a bit of pleasure and lifted it to his lips. He tapped it against the firm line of his mouth as he smiled. Then, licking the digit, he let it drop. Aeron felt the caress as if it had been against her clit. Bron radiated potent sexuality.

"Explore?" Aeron shivered. Had she just said that?

He grinned. By all the stars in the galaxy, that look was incredibly sexy. "If you wish."

Aeron glanced at the bed to where he'd laid the straps and then to the opening of the tent. "No one will come?"

Bron leapt onto the bed in one graceful movement. The loincloth righted itself, hiding his arousal from view as it fell into place. Seconds later he was on his back, arms and legs spread, ready to be tied. "No one will come unless I summon them."

Aeron bit her lip, considering his words. When would she get another opportunity to touch a man? Especially a man who looked as good as this one did? A man whose customs didn't allow him to finish what they started? When would she get to look at one up close without fear of it going too far? Maybe they could play, just a little. She was allowed to seek pleasure, just not sex. Before she fully finished the thought process, she was tying up one of his wrists to the corner post of the bed. He didn't resist.

When she'd bound the remaining limbs, leaving him vulnerable to her whims, she stepped back to admire her work. Muscles strained bronzed flesh, just as his arousal strained the fur loincloth. His hips adjusted beneath the material, moving erotically back and forth in invitation.

A little dizzy from nerves, she went to the food table and grabbed the pitcher of wine and poured a generous amount into the goblet. The strong liquor burned a little, much more potent than the berry wine from the feast. She coughed, but managed to finish the whole goblet. Aeron welcomed the numbing fire unfurling in her stomach and throat.

Lowering her chin, she considered where she was. The man on the bed watched her with a strange mix of anticipation and patience. She moved along the edge of the tent, careful not to step too close to the torches. The firelight only added to the surreal scene, as it danced along the

HIS HIGHNESS THE DUKE

walls. As she passed by the straps, she grabbed a long one, considering blindfolding him so she didn't have to stare into those dark, penetrating eyes.

Aeron continued around the tent to the bath. The water was still hot and she wondered at it as she watched the steam curl and dissipate. Seeing a bottle of rubbing oil, she grabbed that as well. By the time she traveled around the entire tent to stand at the end of the bed, he was breathing hard. His eyes narrowed. There was a predatory intensity to his expression.

"Undress for me," he ordered. Then, as if trying to amend the harsh tone, he added, "please."

Aeron put the bottle of oil by his feet, moved toward the head of the bed, and laid the strap over his eyes. He instantly sensed what she was about to do and lifted up. She tied it loosely around his head.

"If you will not undress yourself, undress me," he said as she tightened the knot against his temple. When she was done, he dropped his head back down on the mattress.

Now that he couldn't watch her with those intense eyes, she went to the bottle and opened it. His muscles tightened, flexing and releasing. He breathed in deeply, as if he could already smell the oil. She touched the arch of his foot and his leg jerked as if she'd burned him. Aeron became

MICHELLE M. PILLOW

bolder, dripping oil on his skin. No one would know. No one would care. Bron was willing. She was willing. She risked nothing by satisfying her curiosity.

Fingers glided over taut flesh. Though her hands were rubbing his legs, her eyes were on his manhood. She watched it for movement. A low moan escaped him as she pushed her hands higher. Liquor curled through her veins, lightening her head until she couldn't think past the moment.

Her body ached for more contact. Aeron's hands met the fur of his loincloth. His hips lifted toward her, rocking gently, up and down, up and down, in an agonizingly seductive rhythm. A glance at his handsome face told her he was still blindfolded. She pulled at the fur, slowly stripping it from him. She knelt between his thighs. Her hands were still slick with oil as she touched his shaft.

"Ah!" He jerked hard.

Aeron smiled, enjoying her new toy. She'd seen pictures, but never one up close, in the flesh. She traced her finger along the head before moving down the shaft to the root. Stroking it harder, she pulled her hand up. His hips lifted off the bed.

Aeron's breathing deepened, taking in the musk of oil and the fresh scent of his skin. Her clothes felt tight so she pulled the gown off and tossed it aside. Getting more oil, she rubbed it on her sensi-

HIS HIGHNESS THE DUKE

tive breasts. Trails of the liquid ran down her stomach. She felt each one like a caress.

"Untie me." Bron groaned.

She leaned over him to wipe her dripping stomach against his. Instead, his shaft was in the way and she ended up sliding against the length of it. Aeron's entire body jolted with awareness and pleasure. She kept her body down, pushing up his chest. Her breasts dragged along him until their nipples touched. Oh, but it felt glorious, unlike anything she'd ever tried. She did it again. And again. And again. And again.

Her breathing became ragged. Bron moved beneath her, helping her to slide. Her legs worked over his hips so she could feel the hard ripple of his stomach along her sex. The sensation was nothing like when she pleasured herself. She moaned softly, running her hands over his chest and neck, shoulders and arms.

"Untie me," he said, this time louder.

She didn't listen. Her butt slid against his shaft, opening her up to a myriad of new sensations. Aeron lifted her hips, angling her body so that her sex pressed tightly against his. It felt as if his body had been created to fit hers. She gasped, rocking along his shaft. It glided in her natural cream.

"Aeron, we must not," Bron gasped, even as his

body moved in rhythm to hers. "We must… tradition."

The friction of his rod against her clit was too much. She felt the pleasure building. She wanted more, needed more. Her hands dug into his chest as she braced herself.

Bron growled. The skin beneath her hands hardened, turning a dark brown. A line grew out from his forehead, pushed forward to make a hard plate of impermeable tissue over his nose and brow. Talons grew from his nail beds and deadly fangs extended from his mouth. With supernatural strength, he ripped through the binds on his arms. Aeron stopped moving, teetering on the edge of pleasure. Excitement pumped through her veins to see the shift in him. He tore the blindfold from his head. His eye yellowed, the darkness in them disappearing.

"What are you?" she whispered, awed by the change in him. Her nails scratched his chest but the new texture was as hard as metal.

As fast as it came, the shifted form left. Her nails bit into his chest and her hands molded into his skin. His voice hoarse, he answered, "Dragonshifter." But his concentration wasn't on his words. He grabbed her hips and lifted her. Aeron felt herself on the brink of pushing down. A moment of confusion passed between them. The length of his shaft found it's opening, probing just inside the depths.

Something rational tried to work its way into her brain, but the thought never fully formed. Everything centered on that moment and the next blissful sensation. At the same second he closed his eyes and pulled her down onto his shaft, she released the tension in her legs and pressed down to take him in. The thick probe of his shaft stretched her.

Aeron moaned. He rocked gently, still holding on to her hips. Her body had been teased to the point of explosion, and now the rocking pressure of him inside her pushed her over the edge. She gave a soft cry as she climaxed. It was unlike anything she'd ever felt. Her muscles squeezed him tight as her entire length tensed. He lifted her a little bit and then dropped her down. Bron jerked with release, joining her climax. Time refused to move and they stayed frozen in that position for a long time. It was perfection.

THE GODS WERE GOING to curse them.

What had he done? Their marriage was cursed.

Bron stared at Aeron's face, watching the ultimate pleasure become replaced by stunned horror.

She must have felt it, too. They were not supposed to fully join this night. The Breeding Festival was meant as a night of discovery only. If the others found out what they had done, his honor would be tarnished. Bron closed his eyes. His honor was already tarnished. *He* knew what they'd done.

Aeron slowly pulled off his body. "What have I done?"

Bron instantly rolled to sitting, cupping her face in his hands to stop her when she would get of the bed. She paused, looking at him. Her pale face and stricken expression tore at his insides, compounding his guilt. She was his bride. She had every reason to trust him to protect her and he'd failed. First, he'd been so preoccupied trying not to hope for a bride that he'd missed her in the receiving line. Then, he didn't try harder to explain about the removal of the mask when she asked him if *he* could remove it and not be married. He should have clarified that if *she* removed the mask it would bind her to him no matter what happened, but he'd been desperate to seal their union. Third, and perhaps the most grievous offense to their now joined honor, was the fact he had taken her fully on their wedding night.

She had only known him for a short time and in that short time he'd failed her, failed himself, failed his family. She'd tested him with her body and he'd failed. The weight of it pressed in on him.

He was the High Duke of Draig, held to the highest of standards. He was to be an example to his people. Perhaps this is why the gods made him wait so many years for a bride. They knew he was not worthy. They knew he would fail. And finally, after all that waiting, he'd proven the fears of the gods right. He failed.

Failed.

No wonder she was looking at him like that. She had bound herself to a man with tarnished honor. She had trusted him.

Failed.

"I will set this right," Bron swore. He brushed the hair from her face as he held her cheeks in his hands, keeping his eyes on hers. "The gods will not curse us. I will atone. I will make this right. They will understand that I waited so long for you. I will repair my honor for you if it takes the rest of my days, Aeron. I swear it on my life."

She still didn't move. He wasn't even sure she heard him. She blinked once, twice, but that was it.

"Remain here." He wanted to kiss her, but he didn't dare. "I will come back for you in the morning. I will take care of everything. I will make this right."

Bron grabbed his loincloth and hurried from the tent. He wasn't sure how he would keep his promise, but he would find a way. By all the gods, he would find a way.

AERON VAGUELY HEARD Bron speaking to her before he left the tent. She sat on the bed, stunned, horrified, terrified. Her hand moved to cover her stomach. The pleasure of Bron's touch had been too much to resist. She couldn't stop herself. She'd been possessed. It felt unlike anything she'd ever experienced, and now the residual pain of their joining was an all too real reminder of her impending death.

Mortality. It wasn't something she was supposed to face. That was why women from her planet—make that her exploded non-existent planet—used transmitters to exchange pleasure essences. She and Riona were the last of their kind. The only men in the universe who understood her biological clock were dead.

"And I'm about to join them," she whispered. Tears entered her eyes. "I'm dying."

She glanced around when no one answered. Bron had left her and she desperately wanted him there to hold her, to somehow reassure her. Yes, he was a stranger, but he was the only thing she had. She thought of her sister, but Riona would provide little comfort. She might understand, but the woman would merely mock her or, worse, look at her with pity.

The empty tent provided little solace. Crying harder, Aeron collapsed onto the bed. "What have I done? What have I done?"

5

Bron knelt in the dark temple, unmoving, arms outstretched, until dawn peeked through the narrow stone window. Even then, as his arms dropped from exhaustion, did he remain, until the sunlight traveled down the wall to hit upon his face. His mind replayed the events of the evening, of his failures, over and over again.

His knees ached when he finally stood, but he ignored the discomfort. He wanted to go to Aeron, but first he needed to make an appearance at the preliminary showing before the king and queen. Many of the grooms did not make it to that part of the traditional ceremony. The elders tended to look the other way at the absences, but Bron was not about to allow another slip in propriety.

The three suns were shining brightly on the red

Qurilixian soil. The soft green sky began to replace the darkness. Knowing where the servants would keep the clothing, he made his way through the forest, over yellow fern groundcover and fallen colossal leaves. Small animals shifted the ferns from beneath. He sensed rather than saw them. A purple bird flew nearby. The supply tent looked like the others without a banner to signify a family line. No one questioned him as he entered, found his clothing and quickly slipped into it. He left the loincloth behind, as he would no longer need it. The loosely fitted, black pants and dark red tunic shirt, though nicely made, were more in line with what he wore every day. Gold embroidered trim decorated the shirt's edges. It was the first time he'd worn the garment and it felt a bit tight around his shoulders. Before he left, he ordered a man to bring Aeron the gown he'd ordered made eight years ago for a new wife. It matched his clothing.

The brides were still sleeping. It was expected they would be absent this morning if the men had done their duty by them. The thought caused Bron to look down at his crystal. Luckily it still glowed. Had it stopped there would have been no hope for him.

Seeing the councilmen gathered around his uncle, the king, he nodded and took his place in line. He wondered if they knew his shameful secret,

HIS HIGHNESS THE DUKE

if they could detect what he had done. Other new husbands stood proudly, waiting to be acknowledged. Like most Draig ceremonies this one would be short. Bron did not see his brothers in attendance, nor three of the four princes. Prince Ualan grinned at him. Bron nodded once as he stood next to him.

"Many blessings, cousin," Bron said.

"Many blessings," Ualan answered. The man could barely contain his excitement. "It is a fine morning, is it not? Though I see our younger brothers did not make it out of bed."

"The burden of being oldest," Bron answered. It was an old joke between them. Ualan was the oldest prince and heir to the throne. They understood each other. They both had high expectations placed on them as the first born sons.

"One that does not seem so heavy today. We are truly families blessed," said the prince.

Before Bron could answer, a councilman called to the line of new husbands, "Lord Ualan?"

"It's done." Ualan stepped forward, lifted his hand high to the council to show the glowing crystal before turning to show it to all gathered. The council acknowledged in silent approval of him and waited for the next man to step forward. Ualan left the area.

Bron, being next in rank followed his cousin's

example. Nervously, he took the crystal from his neck, praying it wouldn't stop glowing as he held it above his head. "It is done." The words were not as strong as Ualan's had been, but they were loud enough. The elders nodded in acknowledgement. Bron turned to go, sighing with relief. The only thing left was to present his bride, and then they could go home and he could find a way to restore his honor, but more importantly, he could begin to make it up to his wife.

AERON TOOK A DRINK OF WINE, wishing it were water but not really caring. She was thankful for the torches, though their low flame was no longer needed. Without them, she would have spent the night alone in the alien darkness. Bron had not returned to the tent. The fact stung, though not as badly as the reason for his going. In one second she had changed everything. Her life was over.

When she closed her eyes, she remembered the look on his face, the hesitance in his expression as she stayed poised over him. He had wanted to stop her. His people's traditions demanded she stop. But she'd been the one in control of the situation. She'd been on top of him, rubbing against him, feeling him, needing him. The memory of it caused an

HIS HIGHNESS THE DUKE

ache to build inside her. She wanted him again. She wanted the sensations, the feelings, the mindless everything.

And yet with the idea of pleasure came an even more real torment. Mortality. She was dying. Her mother had never explained the full bittersweet reality to her. Perhaps she'd been too young to understand it. To experience such deep pleasure, surely what was the pinnacle of what life had to offer, was to court death.

What had been an eternity was now summed up into a few short years. Aeron felt a panic inside her. There wasn't much time left. There was so much she needed to do, needed to say and see and be. She began to pace the tent, pulling at the arm straps hanging from her waist. There hardly seemed enough hours in the day now. How would she fit it all in?

"My lady, may I enter?"

Aeron nearly screamed at the male voice. Her heart was beating so fast. "Yes?"

She recognized the servant from the night before. He was carrying a red bundle in his arms. Seeing her, he bowed his head. "My lady's gown."

Aeron took it from him and said nothing. She wondered if he knew what she'd done. Logic told her she wouldn't look or smell or *be* different, but still the knowledge of it burned so brightly in her mind she was sure everyone else would automatically sense it. He left without comment.

She laid the gown on the bed and went to the tub. The water wasn't as hot as the night before, but she didn't care as she quickly cleaned the restless night from her skin. The deep red of the gown was a strange color choice for her, but then she was only used to wearing Federation black. The bodice had a loose fit and the skirt was about two inches too long. Still, the gold embroidery along the edges was beautiful. Were the stitches meant to symbolize stylized dragons? She couldn't be sure.

Thinking of dragons only made her think of her shifter lover, which made her remember pleasure, which made her remember death, which made her…

"You are beautiful, my lady."

The sound of Bron's voice knocked every thought from her head. She turned to him. He was in a matching red tunic with a large dragon emblem sewn on the chest. The styles of the clothing were similar in cut, clearly made as a set. In a strange way it made her feel as if she belonged to him. "Thank you."

He stood in front of the front flap, not making a move to come inside the tent. His gaze roamed her face, searching her. When neither of them spoke, he moved toward the food table and poured a

HIS HIGHNESS THE DUKE

goblet of wine. Aeron touched her damp hair, quickly smoothing it with her hands. Then, seeing a comb, she made fast work of the long length.

Bron sipped the liquor. He leaned back against the table, watching her pull at her hair. The silence became unbearable and she tried to think of anything she could to fill it.

"Did you sleep well?" she inquired. It wasn't what she wanted to know. What did he think about what happened? How did she do?

How did I do? Aeron grimaced. Was she really looking for a performance review from the man she'd tied up and forced her virginity upon?

"I did not sleep." He set the goblet down on the table. "I was in the temple trying to atone for what happened."

"Atone?" she repeated. It wasn't exactly the thing a girl waited to hear from her first lover.

"I know one night cannot make up for what happened, but I assure you I will restore our family's honor if it takes a lifetime." Bron made a move to take the goblet, but stopped mid-action. Instead, he came toward her. "The activities of last night were not as I intended."

She was about to answer, but the crystal around his neck began to glow and she forgot what she was going to say. Its pulsing light mesmerized her.

Bron followed her gaze down. "We should

finish this before the crystal gets too impatient and enthralls us both. Come."

"Where?"

"I must present you to the council as my wife." Bron picked up her hand in his.

"I can't be your wife. I told you I was not here to marry." Aeron again looked at his crystal. It was so pretty. She wanted to touch it.

"Considering what was done here, I think it is a little late for that," he said. "You are my wife. The rest of the morning is merely a formality. "

"No, you don't understand. I came here to talk to someone about the ore mines." She pulled her hand from his. The physical contact only made it hard to think. "I can't be married."

"There will be time for that after we finish the ceremony and go home."

"Home?" she repeated. "My home is on a spaceship orbiting a military base."

"Your home is in my castle."

"This is not acceptable. I need time to think. Everything is rushing around in my head and—"

"Come to the presentation with me. Finish the ceremony. Then, afterwards, I promise we will discuss the ore, your home, anything that you wish." He sighed. "Please, I ask you, do this. After last night... Please, help me finish the ceremony. It is a matter of my family's honor."

He seemed so earnest that all she could do was nod her head in agreement. "All right. We'll do the ceremony and figure this mess out later."

The tension in his arms lessened. "Thank you, my lady."

Bron couldn't help but notice the glazed look in Aeron's eyes. Her will, as well as her attention, was captured by his crystal. He understood because he too felt the pull. It convinced him all the more that she was meant to be his wife. Even now he wanted to touch her, to pull her back into the tent, into the bed, into his arms.

He led her to the platform where the councilmen stood around royalty. The king and queen were both in regal purple and wore their crowns. They were seated in the center of the platform on thrones.

Bron paused, turning to her. "What is your family name? Your people?"

"Ah, oh, Aeron Grey. My people are," she hesitated.

When she didn't finish, he took her arm in his. To his aunt and uncle, he said, "Queen Mede, King Llyr, may I present Lady Aeron Grey."

"You must be eager," the king said, laughing. "You are the first to arrive."

The queen began speaking in the Qurilixian tongue to her husband. Bron hid his smile. When she finished, the king looked properly chastised, though hardly sorry for his teasing. Queen Mede was a rare Qurilixian-born woman, but that was not how she came to be married to the king. Their match was fated just as everyone else's was.

"Proceed," the queen ordered.

Bron bowed, took the crystal from his neck and handed it to Aeron. She stared at it, rubbing the glowing stone. "Break it."

"But," she whispered, "it is so pretty."

"Smash it," Bron insisted.

She frowned at him and curled her fingers around the stone. "I don't want to. I want to keep it. It's pretty."

"High Duke?" the queen asked.

"One moment," he said. The crowd that gathered to watch began to chuckle and whisper amongst themselves. He grabbed Aeron's wrist and hissed into her ear. "What are you doing? We are in public. Smash the crystal!"

"No!" she protested, trying to get her wrist free. "Let go. I want to keep it."

"God's Bones! Smash the crystal, Aeron." Bron swore, well aware that those around them could probably tune in to every word. Glancing up, he saw the shift of yellow in the council's eyes. Yes, they were definitely listening in.

Bron squeezed the tendons in her wrist forcing her to loosen her hold. Shaking her hand, he made her drop the crystal. Aeron gasped in protest and moved to pick it up from the red earth with her free hand. He pulled her captured hand higher, stopping her. Aeron's eyes met his as she was forced to stand tall. He expected her to fight him. Instead, she smiled. The look momentarily took him off guard.

Aeron took advantage of his stunned state. Lifting on her toes, she grabbed his face with her free hand and kissed him. The crowd laughed and cheered, calling out provocative suggestions to the couple. Bron detected the faint smell of liquor on his people and knew they were still rowdy from the night before. And Aeron was giving them a show.

He was about to pull her away when her tongue touched his lips. He realized this was the first time they'd really kissed. A low moan left him. He felt the crystal pulse at his feet, as if it cocooned them in its power. His hand loosened on her wrist. Her fingers wound into his hair, pulling him closer.

"Lord Bron." The queen's voice came from outside the fog of his pleasure so he ignored it. "High Duke!"

MICHELLE M. PILLOW

Aeron's kiss deepened. Her mouth slid against his, instinctively finding a sweet rhythm with his mouth. Her body slid next to his suggestively.

A hand bit into his arm and shook him hard. "Bron, control yourself, son." Bron jerked his mouth from his wife. The king glared at him. In their shared language, he said, "Make her finish it. Now."

Aeron's mouth moved along his neck and jaw, trying to entice him back to her kiss. Bron fought her spell. He kicked the crystal toward her foot. It hit the side of her slipper. Taking her arms, he lifted her and dropped her foot lightly on the crystal. It shattered like glass.

The laughing crowd cheered, some of them making sounds of disappointment that the show was over. Bron ignored them.

"Bron?" Aeron looked down at her foot and then to him. Confusion filtered through her gaze. Her eyes began to clear of the crystal's influence. She swayed weakly and he had to hold on to her to keep her upright.

The Queen announced, as was customary, "Welcome to the family of Draig, Lady Aeron. I hope you will enjoy your new home."

The marriage was complete.

"Follow me," the king snapped to his nephew.

Bron had no choice but to follow his uncle from

the platform into the surrounding forest. When they were away from prying ears, Bron said, "My king, I can explain."

"I know what you have done," the king said.

"King?" Aeron repeated, her words mumbled. "I needed to speak to the king. It's important."

King Llyr frowned. Leaning over he plucked a green plant with a yellow center from the forest floor.

"I must speak to you, king," Aeron continued to mumble, her words slurred and unsure. Bron pulled her next to him.

The king walked to her, lifted the plant between two fingers and he rubbed them beneath her nose, crushing the little buds.

"I…" Aeron blinked as she inhaled the plant. Instantly, she passed out.

"Get yourself under control," the king ordered now that Aeron was quiet.

"Do not look at me like that, son. I know what you have done and I suspect the council knows as well. You took her last night. That is why she responded to the crystal the way she did," said the king. Bron lifted his chin, careful to keep a hold on Aeron as she slumped against him. "I won't have our family name soiled by an unhappy marriage. There are those who wish to see our line ended. After my sons, you are my heir. I will not grant the

Var the pleasure of seeing our family name tarnished."

"Yes, my king." Bron answered, ashamed that the man knew his secret.

"Take her away from here before she awakens," King Llyr ordered. "I do not know how she will react now that the crystal is broken. The effects might linger for hours or days or even years. A man can well handle a doting wife, but not one who follows him around like a lovesick solarflower after the sun. The traditions are in place for a reason. Get her to your home and make this right with the gods. Or, better yet, take her to the north cabin. There is no reason why you must return home so quickly. Your brothers can manage without you. Whatever duties arise in your absence will be secondary to this problem."

"Yes, my king." What else could he say?

The king sighed. "I may be king but I am still your uncle and the only father you have left in this life. I understand the temptation of our brides and you were made to wait a long time for yours. Such will be taken into account when considering your honor. Go. Take her. Figure this out. I will tell your brothers you are well and will return home in your own time. The fewer who discover this lapse in judgment the better. The groom will bring your mount from the stables and meet you near the

HIS HIGHNESS THE DUKE

twisted tree where you boys used to practice throwing knives."

"Yes," Bron whispered. He lifted his unconscious bride in his arms and moved to take her through the forest.

6

If the rocking didn't stop she was going to be sick. Why didn't the pilot use the atmospheric stabilizers? Aeron moaned, blinking heavily. Bright light invaded her lids, blinding her to her surroundings. The rocking continued, a steady back and forth, back and forth, back and…

"Blast the stars," she moaned, jerking up as nausea rose in her throat. Consciousness came as she was sliding off the back of a giant horned beast. Rough terrain passed by her vision. Her arms flailed, but she didn't find anything to hold on to. A startled scream escaped her lips. Nothing made sense.

A hand grabbed hold of her waist to keep her steady, jerking her upright. She gave a shorter, softer shout of surprise. A voice soothed, "Easy."

It took her brain all of two seconds to place Bron's voice. It took her body exactly two seconds after that to react to it. Desire shot through her like an electrical shock. She became aware of his hand on the side of her gown. The material offered little protection from his heat. Her sleep-hazed mind refused to focus and concentrate.

The rocking wasn't a ship, but a giant beast of a creature they rode on. Bron sat behind her, his chest near her arm. His spread thighs gripped the beast as her legs fell to one side. The wide back of the animal made it easy to regain her balance. Bron pulled her hip and she slid next to spread legs.

Awareness shot through her like a comet and it took her a long moment before she could speak. "What's happening?"

As if to answer, the animal hissed its long tongue. Aeron jumped back, pressing tight into Bron's chest. She drew her legs up in a defensive gesture. His grip tightened on her, steadying her once more.

"What is this thing?"

"It's called a ceffyl. It's harmless," he assured her. "My brother, Alek, breeds them. This one is completely domesticated."

The creature hissed again. It was perhaps the ugliest thing she had ever seen.

HIS HIGHNESS THE DUKE

"I'll take your word for it," she said, not able to fully relax. "Make it stop."

Bron reached around her for the center horn. He gave it a gentle tug. The beast stopped moving. Aeron pushed off its back. Bron's hand slipped from her waist. Her unsteady feet landed on the ground and she stumbled before catching herself.

They were on a wide red-gray path. Mountain peaks grew in the distance, creating a spectacular view. Their jagged tops reached toward the sky like the tops of hand-carved spears. The higher the peak, the grayer they became until there was no red tint left in the earth at all. The air felt thin as she took a deep breath and then another. She couldn't tell if it was the elevation or the memory of Bron's hand on her waist that made her so weak. Regardless, at least the rocking had stopped.

"Hey, easy," Bron said, dismounting. His hand gently touched the small of her back as she leaned over. The ground swam beneath her and she closed her eyes tight. "Try to slow your breathing."

"Where... am... I?" she gasped.

"We're about a day's ride from the palace," Bron answered. "We'll be at the north hunting cabin soon. Everything you need will be provided for you there."

"No, that's..." She frowned, trying to piece together the events of the last day. She'd spent the night alone in a tent. She remembered walking through a fog. It was impressions more than solid memories—Bron's eyes and lips, a glowing stone, the sound of laughter, and dizziness, so much dizziness. What was she now doing in the mountains? She should be by the festival grounds, or on the ship heading away from this planet.

"This is all wrong. I'm not supposed to be here." She looked at his confused expression, stepping away from him. "I need to speak to the king. I need to get back to the Galaxy Brides' ship—oh, no, the ship! I missed the ship."

Aeron looked at the sky, but only saw the narrow streaks of clouds in the green tinted heavens. Undoubtedly her sister had gotten back on the luxury craft without her. Riona would have been stupid not to. There was no telling how Aeron would get off the planet now. The travel arrangements were Riona's specialty. What did Aeron know of making shady deals with space captains and pirates? For who else would give a ride to a Federation analyst who had abandoned her commission and would most likely have a galactic report issued on her name? Federation protocol when they located her abandoned ship would have been to issue a watch for her. She doubted she warranted much of a capture reward, not like a field agent gone rogue, but she did have knowledge

HIS HIGHNESS THE DUKE

of sensitive intergalactic information. She was sure she could work out her job situation with her supervisors when she returned. It would be a mar on her record and there would be quite a bit of explaining to do, but in a few years' time, life would be back to normal. Either that, or they'd no longer require her services and she'd be exiled to some dive fuel docking station as a landing control technician.

"Did you leave something behind? Whatever it is, I will have it replaced for you." Bron made no move to touch her and she was glad for it. "You will want for nothing."

"You speak as if you expect me to stay here with you." A strong breeze came up behind her, sending a chill over her as it molded her long gown to the back of her body. She lifted her arm to keep the hair from her face.

"Of course you will stay with me. You are my wife." His entire body tensed.

"Wife?" She shook her head in denial. "No, that can't be."

His expression dared to disagree.

"I've made a mess of this, haven't I? I wasn't supposed to get married. Maybe I drank too much wine?" She frowned, trying to figure out her situation more than talking to him. "Regardless, I don't think it is wise to continue on. It is better to stop matters right now, instead of letting it drag on unnecessarily." She turned her full attention to him. "I apologize for not making my position clear during the ceremony. I have no excuse for what I have allowed to happen. But, now, I am thinking clearly and I need you to understand that I cannot stay here, with you, as your wife."

"I'm sorry you feel that way, but your leaving is not an option." He crossed his arms over his chest. "You are my wife, decreed by the gods to be so, and—"

"Wait." She held up her hand, stopping him. Memories of a conversation began to clear. "We did discuss this. You said if I did the ceremony we'd talk about getting me back to my home. I did my part." She mimicked his pose, not liking his heavy-handed tone.

"We are discussing it and your home is my home." Bron dropped his arms and motioned to the animal. "Now that you understand clearly that you are my wife and that you will live with me, we may discuss the ore or whatever else you like."

"This is not a discussion," she countered. "You are dictating to me."

"We will be at the cabin soon. Come." He turned his back on her. "After we are settled, you may ask your questions about the ore."

"No." She refused to move. If he thought she was going to just listen to his orders like some

HIS HIGHNESS THE DUKE

soldier in his personal army, he was sorely mistaken.

"Aeron," he paused, softening his tone. "My lady, come. We cannot stand out here all day. I would sleep and bathe. It has been a long ceremony and neither of us is of the temperament to—"

"No." She shook her head, keeping her arms locked across her chest. "I refuse to go with you. You go sleep, and bathe, and find your temperament. I'm going back to the palace. I'll talk to the king and get this marriage terminated. After I tell him why I have come to this planet, I'm sure it will be easily done."

At that a small smile lifted the corner of his mouth. Blast it all, but he was a handsome man. Her scowl deepened.

"And you know the way back to the palace?" He arched a brow in challenge. Now that she studied him there was something to his demeanor, a familiar arrogance that came with the promotion of rank. Whatever he did, this man had power and respect. The knowledge made her nervous, like when she had to face a Federation Military officer or one of the Human Intelligence Agency directors. She hated giving her reports for that very reason.

"I'll manage," she said, not as forceful as before.

MICHELLE M. PILLOW

"Without a ceffyl? By foot? You have knowledge of our wilderness?" His expression only grew more confident.

"You are… This is…" She hesitated, looking around the rough terrain wondering if she had the courage to manage it alone. "This is kidnapping."

At that he laughed. "You agreed to marry me. I cannot kidnap my own wife."

"Well, it's a wifenapping, or some kind of napping," she countered. "My sister will contact the authorities if I'm not returned to the palace."

He appeared completely unconcerned. "Galaxy Brides? They assured us your contracts were in order. You contracted to be a bride, I chose you, you chose me, it is done."

Blast!

He was right. Riona had forged contracts in her name to be a bride. She thought briefly about turning her sister in, but then, it would be hard to prove when she had taken the ride on the Galaxy Brides' ship. And, no matter how frustrating Riona could be, Aeron would never get her into legal trouble. Riona had been doing her a favor.

"No," she countered, "the Federation Military."

"They have no jurisdiction here," he dismissed, completely unmoved by her threats. If anything, he seemed slightly amused by them.

"But they do over me," she answered. "I work

for them. It's my job. They'll miss me if I don't return. They probably have someone coming to find me even now."

"Perhaps, but they have no jurisdiction on this planet, and they won't wish to compromise their ore deliveries by creating an incident. We have dealt with the Federation in the past. Our negotiations with them are clear. They need what we have too much to risk upsetting us." He motioned her to follow. "Come. The cabin is close and will be stocked with food."

Aeron considered her options but still didn't want to follow him. Aside from his highhanded manners, she didn't sense danger in him. In fact, if their night of passion was anything to go by, he was more in danger from her. Just thinking of it made her want to touch him again. She closed her eyes and took a steadying breath. There was really no reason why she shouldn't. The damage had been done.

Bron sighed. "If we went back to the palace, there wouldn't be another ship for quite some time. Even if I was inclined to let you go, there is nowhere for you to go. The king is celebrating the marriages of his four sons. He will expect us to have given the marriage a solid try before he would even consider dissolving it. You are recognized as my wife, so it falls to me to take care of you. No one will take you in. You will have no place to live but with me."

"Why would the king care about your marriage?" she asked, wishing the details of what had happened were clearer. Instead her mind gave her images of sex with Bron, glowing crystals and the feeling of being completely under his spell.

"He is my uncle," Bron said. His eyes narrowed. "So you see, our marriage is not so easy to terminate. The king will not go against the will of the gods, nor will my uncle go against my desire to have a wife. We have the customs for a reason, to be sure we understand the will of the gods. The crystal glows, a woman freely removes the mask, signifying her acceptance, the couple show intent before the council of elders by breaking the crystal. Once the crystal is broken, the binding cannot be easily undone."

A flash of memory filtered through her mind. She frowned, rubbing her temple. She remembered meeting the king. He'd been a stern man of very little humor. In fact… "The king drugged me, didn't he? I remember the king doing something to me when I tried to talk to him."

"It's a plant that grows in the forest. When a person breathes in a high dose of the fresh pollen, it renders them unconscious. Even small children know not to fall down in the yellow fields," he

HIS HIGHNESS THE DUKE

explained. "It is not dangerous in small doses, so long as your enemy is not nearby. The king only wished to help you relax. You were, ah, showing your agreement to the marriage quite enthusiastically."

Aeron remembered just how *enthusiastic* she had been. Considering her situation, she wasn't left with much choice. The king had drugged her when she tried to speak. Galaxy Brides had no incentive to come for her, and the Federation would probably do little to help her, especially when she'd disregarded their order when they told her not to worry about warning the Qurilixian people.

"Fine. I will go with you to the cabin, but only because I have no choice at the moment. This conversation is not over." She began to walk, not wanting to crawl back on top of the large ceffyl beast. Though she intended to let the matter be, she couldn't stop herself from saying, "And I asked you if the mask could be removed without signifying marriage and you indicated it could."

"It could," he affirmed warily. "Eventually."

"So you admit you tried to trick me into removing your mask?"

"I did not trick you. You asked. I answered. Should the night have passed, I could have removed my mask by my own hand after the dawn and we would not be married." He paused, grab-

MICHELLE M. PILLOW

bing the ceffyl by the horn and tugging gently to get it to walk. "You removed it before. The marriage is done, Aeron, and you are my wife. The matter has been discussed at length. Let us speak of the ceremony no more."

Aeron frowned at his back. She considered running. But to where? Who would help her? The Draig king had drugged her. Galaxy Brides was on their way back to whichever spaceport they came from. Riona was undoubtedly with them having a great laugh about Aeron's marriage to a primitive male on the edge of nowhere.

A hollow feeling formed in the pit of her stomach. She was trapped. Here. On this primitive planet about to be attacked by the much more advanced Tyoe with a man who did not love her, could not love her. They had just met. Logically, his interest in her was purely procreational. Oh, and even better, Bron seemed to have the impression that he could dictate to her exactly what she would and would not talk about.

"I'm going to die without ever having lived," she whispered, looking up at the wide universe beyond her vision. Suddenly, she felt the appeal of Riona's carefree life and all of the whims she'd had since childhood flooded in. There was so much she'd wanted to do and try but she'd been too scared to actually live. So she had locked herself away in a metal box and hid. "I thought I'd have more time."

Bron glanced back at her, but she pretended not to notice. Her words weren't meant for him anyway.

BRON DID NOT like how his first day of marriage was progressing. His bride spoke as if she had been taken against her will. Every time he opened his mouth to speak to her, he felt as if he was dictating to a servant. No, actually, he usually sounded less harsh with his servants. He just couldn't seem to help himself with her. She tried to get out of their marriage and his first reaction was to order her to stay. He was a warrior, a leader. It was in his nature to fight and command.

Glancing over his shoulder at his reluctant bride, he frowned. Perhaps his little woman wasn't as breakable as he'd first thought. She seemed to hold her own against him just fine. Then seeing the troubled expression brewing in her gaze, he wasn't so sure. She did look delicate, fragile, even hurt. Had he hurt her? Had he put that look in her eyes?

Bron took a slow, deep breath. What did he know of a woman's moods? He felt his world pulling apart. This was not how things were supposed to be between a man and his woman.

The gods had a plan. He trusted fate, even when it seemed to laugh at his torment. Perhaps his crystal had been damaged? Micro-cracked? Tainted? Had the gods' message for him gone awry because of it?

Why couldn't she just accept their fate? Bron had to believe that the gods would not have willed this union if it was not meant to be. He may have had his doubts over the years, but he knew that much. The whole remembered history of his people proved their traditions had merit.

And, yet, a tiny fear whispered in the back of his mind. What if the gods had not blessed him? What if he was cursed? What if they had merely sent Aeron to him to tell him to give up, to not go to the ceremonies, to live a life alone? They had sent her to break his crystal and then leave him. As the fear grew, he felt himself wanting to hold on tighter. She was his only chance at happiness, at marriage, at children, at love. He had to find a way to please her, so long as it didn't compromise his honor.

She was coming to the north cabin with him. That was a beginning. They would have time alone to sort this out.

Unfortunately, there wasn't much said in Qurilixian tradition about how to restore one's honor after a lapse. Lapse? His failure as a husband was more than a mere lapse. It was a catastrophe. He'd taken his wife before the ceremony was finished. What should have been a time of discovery had turned into a, well, it had turned into something purely fantastic and utterly satisfying in every physical sense. Regardless, physical ecstasy did not excuse his behavior. The reason there was nothing in the tradition about reviving honor was because tradition demanded that they not lose their honor to begin with.

Bron was torn. How could failure still feel so sweet? He'd give anything to touch her again, to kiss her. Perhaps that was his punishment. He'd been weak on the night it mattered most. Now he must be strong until the gods forgave him for that weakness—even if it took months, years, a lifetime. No matter how much he wanted her, no matter the temptation, Bron could not make love to his wife until his honor was restored.

AERON WANTED nothing more than to grab her "husband" and drag him to the rocky ground next to the narrow path to have her way with him. She wanted to feel his fullness again. She wanted to kiss him and touch him and rip his clothes off his body. She refrained, barely, but that didn't stop the thoughts from circling through her brain. Now that she knew what pleasure could be found, she wanted it again, and again, and—*sweet black hole of temptation*—she wanted it yet again after that.

The damage was done. Her fate was sealed. What point was there in resisting what she wanted? And what she wanted was pleasure. She wanted her heart to pound, her breath to catch, and her body to explode and weaken. Oh, and his hands, she wanted to feel those hands on her skin. She had become mesmerized by their strength.

A steep incline forced her back onto the ceffyl. Bron ordered her to hold on tightly to the center horn as he shifted to his dragon form and leapt ahead. The shift should have been frightening, but it wasn't. She remembered all too well the powerful feel of him shifted beneath her thighs.

Bron whistled once and the ceffyl began to climb, moving deftly for its size up the incline in a zigzag pattern. She held her breath and closed her eyes tight as it moved. Only when the ground leveled beneath her did she open them again.

A long building stood at the top of the cliff. The walls were constructed from blocks of gray stone and topped with a flat roof. A dirt path led around the side toward the thick brush. Unlike the

HIS HIGHNESS THE DUKE

forest by the palace, the trees here were skinny with thick willowy tops. Behind her, the view stretched for miles. From this spot, it would be easy for Bron to see her on the trail should she decide to make her way back to the palace alone. Though, even without the view, she imagined Bron would be able to track her quite easily. This was his home world, after all.

At the moment she was too tired to even think of running away. Letting go of the ceffyl's horn, she carefully dismounted and took several steps away from it. The beast ignored her, more interested in the thin slivers of gray-blue grass growing on the ground. It licked at them, twirling its tongue before pulling the blades into its mouth. A low hissing noise sounded as it chewed.

Aeron walked away from the cliff's edge toward the cabin. The stone wall was precisely cut and smoothed. A single plank of wood made the door, the grain spiraling from the middle. Most likely, it was part of a larger tree at the base of the mountains that had been carted up the mountain paths. Bron reached above his head and placed his hand against the middle stone. Seconds later the door unlatched. He hooked the side with his finger and pulled it open.

Aeron looked up as she passed under the hand scanner, but the unit wasn't noticeable. Inside lights from the narrow window streamed in. Bron turned a rectangular mirror mounted on a tall column. It reflected the sunlight onto other strategically placed mirrors higher on the walls and instantly bathed the cabin's interior with light. The entryway led to one large room with three arched doorways. The walls and floor were stone, built from the same kind of precisely cut blocks as the exterior. There wasn't much by the way of décor beyond the fine crafts-manship of the structure. A large fire pit stood barren in the middle of the room. A domed hood hovered high above it, leading up a long column to the ceiling to filter out the smoke. Right now the pit was dormant.

A shadow was cast along the ceiling as Bron walked in front of the reflective mirror. Aeron glanced at him before continuing her exploration. Cushioned furniture surrounded the fire pit. The bases were a combination of stone and wood. A long polished stone table stood at the far side of the room, large enough to seat a dozen people. Benches curved around its oval shape.

"Bathing room," Bron said, motioning to the closest door. "The kitchen is over there on the opposite side and that doorway at the far end leads to the sleeping chambers. Since this cabin is normally used to house hunting parties, there are twelve rooms. You may have your pick of any one, though I might recommend the one at the end of the hall. It is the largest and most comfortable."

"Is that where you will be staying?" she asked, unable to help the small smile forming on her face.

"I will take one of the other rooms," he stated.

At that her smile frowned. "Why? I don't see any logic for it. No matter how this situation is going to end up, we've already been intimate. I see no reason why we don't continue as long as we're together."

The man actually looked shocked at her forward proposal. She wondered if she should fake embarrassment, but really she saw no need to pretend. She was merely stating the logical conclusion to their relationship. The damage was done. They'd found pleasure. It's not like she could get pregnant. The Federation unit she worked for was very strict about issuing their birth control shots and she'd just had hers—even though she'd never found the need for them until now.

"If you are unsure about our marriage, then I think it will be best if we don't—"

"If you wish to stay married to me, you must find me attractive. Have your bodily responses toward me changed?" she countered. "Mine haven't. I find you quite enjoyable to look at. Physical pleasure need not coincide with marital arrangements. I am able to separate the two in my mind. I believe you could come to the same conclusion should you choose to consider it."

He actually looked speechless.

"It's not as if you had never been with a woman before me." Aeron gave him a pointed look and dared him to answer. He didn't move. "I thought so. Our races are different in that regard. I did not anticipate that a man as well," she looked him over, trying to think of a tactful way of saying, *well endowed with obvious sexual appeal and a body that radiated a natural aphrodisiac*. Instead, she said, "that a man with your physical presence would be without female company."

"My company was before I entered into my first ceremony," he tried to answer, only to stop with a pained look. "I do not see how this conversation is relevant to our current situation. Now that we are married, I want no other woman."

"Great, then you admit that you do want me. Should we find one of those rooms?" Ok, so maybe she was being obstinate on purpose. Aeron found she liked him a little speechless. It beat his dictating tone. "Well, you think about it. Last room at the end of the hall is fine with me. I will take your word that it is the best." She began moving toward the kitchen doorway. "Is there a food simulator? I'm famished."

HIS HIGHNESS THE DUKE

"No. We don't require them," he answered. "The larder should be stocked with basic supplies."

"I'll manage. I've taken cooking uploads." Aeron had never really used the cooking skills, but whenever she had downtime, she liked to learn new things. "I cannot guarantee the outcome, but I believe I should be able to make something palatable."

"I will assist you." Bron followed, almost eagerly, as if he were glad to have something to discuss other than sex. She found his reaction curious, considering how open his people were to expressing their primitive physical states. "You will need help with the cooking fire if you have never used one."

Bron lit a fire in a stone oven built into the wall. Hand levers brought down various styles of cook tops from grates to smooth metal. The gentle sound of water from a small indoor waterfall created a constant background to her work.

The problem with uploads was they gave all the information a person needed, but the practical application was somewhat trickier to apply. Aeron knew how to cut the meat Bron supplied for her, but the actual process of it was much more difficult than she'd anticipated. Luckily, Bron was able to provide her with spices and herbs to compliment the meat's natural flavor, otherwise she would have been lost on how to combine their tastes. Cooking was an exact art, one that the uploads only provided vague skills about. Each planet had unique spices and herbs, staples and flavors. Without more specifically detailed instructions into local cuisine, it became a matter of trial, error, success, and instinct. Even with the challenges, she found she enjoyed the creative process.

"Are you looking for something?" Bron asked from the doorway. His hair was wet and combed back from his face. He'd changed his clothes from the ceremonial tunic to slightly less auspicious in design. The loose-fitting pants and long overtunic were crafted from a lightweight, flowing material. As he leaned against the archway, it molded against his hips and chest to give a teasing hint of what lay beneath. She found herself staring at the curve of his hip, forgetting what she'd been doing. "My lady?"

"Ah," she glanced at the food, "something to put this on? A trencher is what the palace servant called it."

Bron nodded, pushing away from the archway. He ran his hand over a sensor near the waterfall. The sensor's design was hidden in the stone wall, completely unnoticeable if a person didn't know where to look. The wall opened and he took out two small, square trenchers for the food. Without waiting for her to ask, he plated the strips of meat and carried them out to the table.

Aeron followed him. Wine goblets had been set out on the table. She caught the scent of soap and eyed his wet hair as he sat down. "This cabin has a water bath?"

"Yes."

She looked down at her gown. It was the same one she'd worn to the crystal breaking ceremony, and then on the journey up. She'd been sitting on the ceffyl. It was not the most pleasant of smelling creature. Slowly, she took a seat, not feeling as confident as before.

"I will show you after we eat," he offered.

"Thank you," she said, reaching for the pronged dining tool. She watched as he tried a strip of meat.

Instantly, a surprised smile crossed his features. "You have a natural talent for food." He quickly took another bite, chewing and nodding his head in approval.

Aeron smiled, pleased by the compliment. She tried a bite. It might have been the work behind it, or just self bias, but she was sure it was better than anything that could come from a simulator.

"You will make me a very fine wife," he continued. "I am pleased. My brothers will enjoy visiting."

Her smile fell. The man didn't seem to listen to her at all, or was just too obstinate to admit defeat. How many times, how many ways, did she need to tell him she was not staying on as his wife? The more confused her situation became, the more she longed for the safe, familiar metal Federation quarters. Even as she thought it, she knew she also longed for adventure. The conflicting desires warred inside her.

She ate in silence. When they were done, she said, "I would like to bathe now and then perhaps sleep."

"Of course." He stood and motioned for her to follow him to the bathing room door. "This way, my lady."

BRON TRIED NOT to think of his wife, her body naked and wet, trailing with soap as she bathed in the cabin's large tub. He *tried* not to think about it, but with every enhanced sense in his body focused on the sounds coming from the bath he couldn't help himself. Water dripped, splashed, stirred. Hands brushed flesh. He heard the slide of them, the silky glide of soap easing the way. Next, a tiny moan, a relaxed sigh, a deep breath, and then the seductive process started all over again.

HIS HIGHNESS THE DUKE

He stared at the stone door frame, able to see each minute grain in the polished gray pattern. His hand lifted and pressed against the stone. Bron caressed the hard surface, running his finger along the curved edge of the frame. She was his wife. He wanted to touch her. He caught her scent, the smell of woman mingling with the bathwater and suds.

By all the gods, he needed to touch her. And yet, he couldn't. Not until he was sure he'd atoned for his sins.

Perhaps bringing her to the privacy of the cabin had been a misguided idea. What else could he have done? He'd been ordered by the king. Yet here, alone with her, hearing the sound of what could only be interpreted as her soapy hands gliding over her body, he could hardly be trusted to atone for anything. The beast inside him raged, wanting him to break down the door and let instinct take over. Her words earlier filled his mind. She wanted him in the most physical of senses. Knowing of her desire, hearing it actually formed into words, had nearly driven him to the brink of sexual madness.

She was his. *His.* And he wanted nothing more than to stake his claim.

His heart pounded, growing so loud it blocked out all other sounds. He breathed hard, drawing in ragged pants. Sweat beaded his brow. Every nerve inside him tingled, threatening with a shift. Knowing he had to put distance between them or risk another disgrace to his honor, he pushed away from the door and practically ran outside. The ceffyl lifted his head and warily eyed Bron's near wild state.

Bron sprinted toward the trees, letting the shift take him so that he could move faster and push his body harder. The sexual desire inside him calmed, but the need did not go away completely. It only became buried beneath the physical shell. Thankfully, the Draig did not take women in shifted form. The fact gave him some reprieve from the ache in his gut.

His heart pounded in a hard steady rhythm and he became aware of his surroundings. Every sound and smell filled his mind, from the tiniest insect to the loudest birds up on the high peak. The mountain peaks surrounded the valley, rising above where the trees would grow. If he ran uphill, he'd find a clearing of rocks where some of the most dangerous creatures on the planet roamed. Rarely was he able to indulge in such pure freedom. Here, he was just a man, unburdened by his title and duty, away from the prying eyes of the people and the threat of their enemies.

The pleasure of the excursion caused him to run faster. In this moment, everything was as it should be. He understood his surroundings. The forest made sense. He knew his body, its limits, and pushed past them. His muscles burned. His heart raced. His mind cleared of all thoughts, but one. Aeron.

7

Gone.

Aeron wasn't sure what to make of being abandoned. She hadn't thought to be worried as she left the water bath to find a bed. She'd assumed Bron merely slept in one of the other bedrooms. The next morning, or at least what she assumed was morning as she couldn't be sure by the constant stream of light coming from outside, he was still missing. After preparing and eating food, she checked the bedrooms. They were empty.

The ceffyl lounged in the lawn, untethered and apparently completely unconcerned with anything beyond licking its own hoof. The expanse of the outdoors made her nervous. She checked around the outside of the cabin, carefully keeping an eye on the nearby forest.

"Bron?" she whispered. Did she dare speak his name louder? What if someone was in the forest? What if they came for her next? Or a hungry animal?

Aeron closed her eyes, recalling some of the uploads. There were allusions to dangerous beasts native to the planet. If a ceffyl was considered tame, then she could imagine what a wild creature would be like.

"Bron?" she said, this time slightly louder. There was no answer.

Aeron scanned the forest floor, trying to find some clue as to where he could have gone. Old leaves and fallen logs intermingled with tiny shoots of the gray and yellow plants. Rocks covered in fine-haired moss jutted from a few places. Nothing she saw indicated Bron had passed by—not that she knew what to look for.

"Come on, Bron," she whispered, growing more frantic by the minute. "I'm not a field agent. Don't leave me alone here. I don't know what to do."

Aeron searched the distance from the cliff, squinting to see down the mountainside. Still, there was nothing. Going back to the house, she tried to wait, pacing the length of the home to look out one narrow window and then another. The skirts of her gown tangled around her legs and she jerked

HIS HIGHNESS THE DUKE

angrily at them as they tripped her. It was the same gown she'd been wearing for days. Without a change of clothes, she had little choice but to wear it again. Minutes turned to what had to be hours, and each passing second caused the knot in her stomach to tighten.

Aeron gathered food supplies, hoping beyond hope that Bron would walk through the door and thus make any attempt at looking for him unnecessary. He didn't and she was forced to brave the mountainside alone. The hazy light cast over her surroundings. At least it would not get dark.

This was not supposed to be happening to her. There had been a calming effect to Bron's presence, overbearing as it was. Now, without him by her side, she felt the full scope of the open terrain.

"You're in a ship. The virtual reality room is really enclosed by metal grated walls that are projecting this impression. Nothing here can hurt me. The computer has safety protocols activated." It was all lies, but it made her feel somewhat better. Aeron made another lap around the house, trying to find clues as to where Bron had gone. Nothing. She secured the makeshift bag she'd created over her shoulder and eyed the ceffyl. "Security protocols are on. Nothing can hurt me."

She stepped toward the ceffyl. It turned its head, eyeing her. A long tongue slithered out and wiggled in the air for several long seconds. Slowly, she reached for the center horn and gave it a small tug. It didn't respond. She did it again, harder, just like Bron had done. Again, it didn't move.

"Fine!" she grumbled. "Stay here. I'm going to find the palace and get some help."

A very ungraceful slide down the cliff saw her to the top of the long mountain path. The skirts of the gown she'd been given to wear after the ceremony offered little protection as they caught on jutted rocks. She had thought about taking some of the male clothing she had found in the home, but couldn't bring herself to take it without permission. The gown would have to do. A stone scraped the back of her calf and thigh, causing a sharp sting to radiate along her leg. This rescue mission was not going well.

Before she could take two steps down the mountain path, she heard hooves sliding. She turned to see the ceffyl standing behind her, eyeing her as if it waited for her to react.

"Oh, now you come," she said. The beast lifted its head and slithered his tongue. Secretly, she was glad for its company. Surely such an unsightly thing would scare off other unsightly things. Aeron focused her attention toward the distance. "Well, come on then, Hideous. We've got a long walk ahead of us."

Nothing. No one.

Aeron kept walking, even when she was tired. The ceffyl followed her, stopped when she paused, moved when she moved, looked at her with its giant reptilian eyes when she ate until finally she set a piece of meat on the ground. She jerked her hand back just as the long tongue shot out to pick it up. She soon discovered the thing would put anything in its mouth, including little rocks it licked up along the trail.

Suddenly, she heard a moan. The almost pained sound jerked her into motion. She rushed forward, up a small incline to see down the immediate path. Bron? It sounded like a man's voice. What was he doing all the way…?

"Oh! Ah!" Aeron gasped in shock. A couple stood on the path, in plain view of anyone and anything, locked in what could only be described as a very intimate, highly inappropriate, private embrace. The woman was partially hidden from view, but it was clear by the tugging motion of her arm that she was in the process of stroking her companion most intimately. The man's position was little better. He had his hand gripping the woman's exposed ass as he held her skirts up.

At her intrusion, the couple stopped kissing and

looked at each other. It took a very long moment for them to turn to acknowledge Aeron. She thought about running, unsure if she should have made her presence known to strangers in the middle of nowhere on an alien planet. But, as she was about to make good her not-so-subtle escape, the trysting woman turned more fully into view. She had blonde hair with red tips and deeply soulful brown eyes. Aeron recognized her from the Galaxy Brides' ship as Kendall Haven. Flustered to be caught staring and yet unable to run away from the first sign of help she'd seen all day, she mumbled, "I… Apologies… Walking…"

It wasn't her most graceful of sentences, but the Draig man was glaring at her like he wanted to attack her for the interruption. Kendall studied her lover's face before glancing down his body to where her hand still rested on his erection. Kendall turned red and she twisted her body away from Aeron to straighten her clothing. The man seemed loath to let Kendall go. His hands were much slower in releasing their hold. Kendall swept her hands over her body to make sure she was covered.

Aeron forced her gaze down and to the side. It was a meaningless gesture, as she'd already seen what they'd been doing. "I didn't mean to intrude." She regained the majority of her senses. Maybe if she ignored what she saw and never mentioned it,

HIS HIGHNESS THE DUKE

they wouldn't either. "I've been walking for a long time."

"Who are you?" the man questioned. "What are you doing with that ceffyl?"

Aeron glanced behind her to the animal following her over the ridge. Her ceffyl caught up to her only to walk down toward the other animal waiting near the couple. The smaller ceffyl lowered its head and moved toward the much larger beast. The two ugly creatures began rubbing horns.

"It followed me," Aeron answered. She looked almost desperately at Kendall for help. The woman wasn't a friend, but she was a welcome face in light of the man's overly harsh tone.

"Alek, this is Aeron. She was on the Galaxy Brides' ship with me," Kendall explained.

"Aeron Grey," Aeron filled in.

"What are you doing out here alone, Aeron Grey?" Alek asked.

Aeron gestured helplessly. The morning had given her ample time to worry about Bron. She might not think to live happily ever after with him, but that didn't mean she wanted him dead or injured. "I don't know."

"Where is your husband?" Alek took a step toward her.

"I'm not really married. I mean, I am, but I'm not. It's hard to explain," Aeron said.

Alek shot a sidelong glance at Kendall. "There seems to be that complication a lot with this shipment."

Kendall looked to the ground and took a step away from him toward Aeron. "What happened?"

"I don't know. There was the ceremony and then the king drugged me with this yellow pollen thing and then I was taken to," she turned and pointed up the mountain, "to this cabin home in the mountains. I took a bath, went to bed, and I woke up alone."

Alek was on her in an instant. "The mountain cabin? What happened? Where is your husband?"

"I…" Aeron automatically tried to get away from the charging man. His dark brown eyes narrowed in on her. Alek grabbed her arm and jerked her forward. His fingers bit into her flesh. "I don't know."

"What have you done?" he demanded, giving her a small shake.

"I did nothing!" she cried. "I woke up and he was gone."

"Who?"

"My husband," she answered, desperately tugging at her arm. It did no good. The more she pulled the tighter his grip became. She looked at Kendall for help, but the woman didn't move. Instead, Kendall stared at Alek with a strange look

HIS HIGHNESS THE DUKE

on her face. "I waited for him for hours, most of the day, but I think he must have gone out the night before and he didn't come back. He didn't say what he was doing. I tried to find him, but it was as if he was just snatched from the ground into the heavens. I couldn't even see footprints."

"Who is your husband?" Alek demanded. And Aeron had thought Bron was high-handed in his manners! This man was infuriating. Only her fear of him kept Aeron from arguing.

"B—Bron," she stammered. "He's the High—"

"I know who he is," Alek snapped. He let go of Aeron's arm. She automatically rubbed the injured appendage. To Kendall, he said, "We must go to the cabin. Bron would not have left her alone. Not for so long. Something must have happened." He looked suspiciously at Aeron. "Or someone did something to him."

There was definitely a difference in him when he looked at Kendall. For Kendall he softened some, even as he sounded gruff.

"I—" Aeron began. His cold, mistrusting look stopped her from finishing.

"We ride to the cabin," Alek ordered.

Kendall frowned. "What about your home? We were going—"

"Our home will have to wait," he broke in. "Get on the ceffyl."

131

Alek forced the ceffyls to run a hard, fast pace. Aeron thought better than to protest. Every time the man looked in her direction, it was to glare. Kendall rode behind him on his larger beast. Her expression seemed worried, only Aeron wasn't sure why.

"Kendall, did you happen to see my sister?" Aeron asked. It had taken her a good portion of the ride to get the courage to speak. Alek tensed, but said nothing. "I am sure she got back onto the ship since she did not find a husband, but I did not have the chance to say farewell to her."

"Riona?" Kendall confirmed. Aeron nodded. "No, I only saw her at the banquet. I'm sorry. I don't know anything."

Aeron nodded again, disappointed but not surprised.

She recognized the terrain as they reached the cabin. Knowing what to expect this time, she held on tight and closed her eyes as the ceffyl took her up the cliff to level ground. Aeron dropped the bag of food on the ground and moved toward the door. "I'll see if he returned while I was gone."

Alek lifted his head and inhaled deeply. "No. he's not here." The man breathed again. His eyes

HIS HIGHNESS THE DUKE

shifted with gold. "I detect his scent in the forest, but it is faint, hours old."

"You can tell that just by smelling?" Kendall asked, surprised.

Alek nodded. "Go inside. Stay here, together. Do not leave the house. I go to look for my brother."

Alek shifted, his body hardening like his eyes as he turned his attention to the mountain forest. The form of the dragon came over him, from the talons on his fingertips to the hard ridge along his forehead. He surged forward, disappearing into a blur within the trees.

"Don't be scared," Kendall said. "The Galaxy Brides' downloads were somewhat incomplete. These men are shifters."

Aeron nodded. "I know. Bron showed me." Then, thinking of just how and when Bron had shown her, she quickly turned toward the cabin. "If I looked worried it was because I couldn't help wondering what we would do if Alek does not come back."

Kendall seemed surprised by the thought and hesitated as she looked to where he'd disappeared into the forest.

"It was just a worry. I'm sure he will return. He seems very taken with you." Aeron managed a smile she didn't feel. A wave of embarrassment

MICHELLE M. PILLOW

washed over her at the idea of Bron abandoning her. She had insisted she was not there to be married. What if he simply took her at her word and left her? Now, Alek was out running in the forest, worried about his brother. She swallowed nervously. "I'm just glad someone else is here to look for him. I didn't know what to do. I don't know anything about these forests, let alone tracking. I'm not even sure how to get back to the palace. I was guessing."

Aeron felt so helpless, and worried, and embarrassed. She'd offered herself to Bron and he'd refused to sleep with her again. Now that Kendall and Alek were helping her, she had time to stop and think about what had happened. How much her life had changed in just a short time.

She led the way into the cabin, turning the light on as Bron had shown her. Without bothering to ask Kendall if she was hungry, Aeron went to the kitchen and began pulling out food. It kept her hands busy and she found she desperately wanted something to do. Besides, assessing the cooking uploads forced her brain to concentrate.

Kendall followed, watching. "You said you're not really married? If you don't plan on being married, why did you get on the ship?"

"It's a long story," Aeron answered. Some field agent she'd turned out to be. Here she was trying to

HIS HIGHNESS THE DUKE

save a people and so far all she managed to do was find a husband she couldn't want. Well, she could and did want him, she just wasn't sure she wanted to spend the rest of her severely shortened life on a primitive planet taking orders from him. "And you? You seemed pretty comfortable with your husband, yet he appeared to be unconvinced of your plans to be his wife."

"It's a long story," Kendall answered.

Aeron gave a short laugh. "Fair answer."

"Alek has his appeal," Kendall explained, "and he did me a great favor, which makes me indebted to him, but I have a family matter that requires I leave."

"And if you could stay, would you?"

Kendall gestured helplessly. "I don't know."

"Bron has his appeal, as well," Aeron said, "when he's not speaking to me as if I am to be ordered about like a servant."

"Must be a family trait." Kendall gave a wry smile. She made her way into the kitchen. "Can I help with something?"

Aeron gave her some quick basic instructions before continuing the conversation. Kendall cut slices of raw meat into thin strips while Aeron boiled water. They talked of the ship, of the other brides, and how strange this new planet of alpha males was compared to the other places they had been.

"I grew up on a fueling dock." Kendall finished cutting one piece of meat and began on the next one. "I'm used to a variety of species, just not the wide open spaces."

"I work in a small metal room." She dropped vegetables into the boiling water, only to snap her hand back when the steam heated her skin. "I'm not used to species or wide open spaces. In fact, I'm not used to conversations that don't include a communicator."

"So, why were you on the Galaxy Brides' ship?"

"It really is a long story. I needed to secure a meeting on this planet and my sister," Aeron paused and gave a small laugh, "my sister was in charge of the travel arrangements. She's a little unconventional when it comes to such things. To tell the truth, she's unconventional when it comes to most things." Aeron realized she was staring toward the door. She drew her eyes away.

"I would tell you that he's fine, but I have no way of knowing if that is true."

"I'll show you how to cook the meat strips." Aeron took the meat and moved toward the cooking fire to lay them out. Then, quietly, she said, "Thank you for the thought. I honestly don't know why I'm worried. This is their homeland. He probably just lost track of time, or was distracted by something important."

"I'm sure that's it," Kendall said, though she didn't sound convinced. Then, wrinkling her nose, she asked, "Is meat supposed to smell like that?"

8

Bron strained against his ties. He wasn't sure who had captured him, but there was one logical answer. The House of Var. King Attor and his cat-shifting race of fanatics made for worthy enemies. They were powerful, ruling over the southern half of the small planet. Many, like Bron's father before he died, believed that they were facing another war with the cat-shifters. Wars were terrible affairs for their kind, lasting sometimes for fifty to a hundred years with many deaths and seldom any clear progress or victory, just an uneasy truce while each side replenished their warriors and concentrated on rebuilding the population. Bron often thought something might happen soon to spark the next war. He considered his lonely prison cell and realized that now was the perfect time for the Var to strike. Seven of the eight noblemen had found brides. Marriage led to children, children grew into power, and so the next generation of fighters would be born. The best way to stop an age-old battle was to ensure the enemy had no future generations to lead or to fight.

Still, even as he struggled against his chains, he couldn't help but feel that his capture was very strange for a man like King Attor. Attor was from the old warrior class. It was not like him to take a prisoner of high worth only to ignore him. If Attor had taken him, he would want everyone to know. Unless he had reason to keep Bron's imprisonment a secret.

At the very, very least, the Var king would want Bron to know who had outwitted him and abandoned him in the ancient dungeon. The fact that Attor did not show himself meant his captors might be coming back for him. They would not leave him to starve, alone, letting his family to forever wonder what happened to him. This was not the Var way. And who else would dare to do this?

Bron frowned, trying with renewed force to free himself. Chains clanked against the metal floors and wall. What if they stole his bride? It would seem suitable punishment by the gods for his dishonoring the ceremony by allowing the consummation of their marriage early. What if someone

HIS HIGHNESS THE DUKE

else wanted Aeron for his own? What better way to stake claim to her than to make it look like he had run out on his marital duties?

What Aeron must think of him! No one would be coming to help them. She didn't know her way around his planet. Even if she was safe, she would be abandoned and alone in the middle of Qurilixen's mountain wilderness. It could be months before his brothers thought to look for him—especially if the king ordered them to leave him be as he atoned.

Bron began to yell, roaring in frustration as he braced his feet against the wall and pulled. The method had not worked so far, neither had trying to pick the locks with his talon, but that didn't stop him from trying. He had to do something. He had to get back to his bride and assure her safety.

"Bron?"

Bron froze, hearing his name. "Alek? Is that you? Have the Var captured you as well? Are you harmed?"

His answer was a loud pounding and scraping. It took several minutes but finally Alek's shifted fingers shot out from behind a thick metal door. He groaned hard, breaking in to where his brother was held captive. "I saw no Var, but that does not mean they are not close. There were boulders against your door. Someone did not want you found."

"Help me with the chains," Bron commanded. They both pulled, using their shifted strength to force the chains free from the wall. They gave with a loud crack of stone. Bron threw the chains over his shoulder, as the cuffs were still attached to his wrists. "How did you find me?"

"Your wife," Alek answered. He slid through the broken door frame and past a large boulder.

"Aeron? Is she all right?"

"I caught her trying to travel down to the palace on your ceffyl." Alek paused, breathing deeply to sense their surroundings. "She is safe."

Bron, realizing they weren't in the best position to discuss anything but making good his rescue, decided not to press the issue of his wife. She was all right. That was all he needed to know at the moment. Tension tightened every muscle in his body. He could detect no one in the immediate area.

Outside his prison was a dark tunnel with light streaming from above. He hadn't realized how dim his cell had been until he saw the bright light. His shifted eyes had seen easily in the dark, but now they ached as they adjusted to the light. He followed Alek, watching his brother's back for guidance.

"Careful," Bron warned. "They disguise their scent. I did not smell them coming for me. I was

HIS HIGHNESS THE DUKE

running and then I was in that dungeon, as if only a second had passed in between."

"How could you not detect their foulness? Has your bride tainted your thinking so much?" Alek asked, his tone hard as they clawed their way up a narrow shaft toward the light.

They appeared on the forest floor. He recognized the smell of the mountain instantly, but he did not know there was an old cave cell beneath the earth. The forest was still but for the gentle call of the birds.

"How did the Var know of this place? We have been all over these mountains and I have never heard of an underground prison."

"It looks to be a relic of the ancient wars." Alek looked around. "They must not have expected anyone to find you. I think they left you to rot." Alek gave him a meaningful look. "I am glad the gods had other plans for you."

"I owe you much, brother," Bron said, by way of a thank you.

Alek nodded once. "It was your bride who alerted me. I may have been harsh with her."

If Alek was worried, it was possible he'd been less than cordial. Bron well understood, though, and was too grateful for his rescue to complain. "I will take care of it. I will make her understand."

"Can you run? I left our brides at the cabin when I came to track you."

Bron answered by leading the way at a full sprint. The thick chains bounced against his back, but the metal didn't hurt his shifted flesh. The sound of Alek's footfalls joined his and they did not speak as they made their way back to the cabin.

AERON COULDN'T FORCE herself to eat as she watched the cabin door. Kendall tried to fill the silence with conversation. They discussed the Galaxy Brides' ship and Kendall's home on a fueling dock. Aeron got the impression that there was a greater story there. When she asked why Kendall had come to the Qurilixen ceremony, the woman artfully changed the subject as she started talking about mining ores and space fuel. Apparently, Kendall was in the process of getting certified by the Exploratory Science Commission as a Fuelologist and Station Engineer. Since she lived on a space fuel port, the certification made sense.

"I'm not sure how much you know about mining," Kendall said, "but this planet is one of the only mineral rich sources of the *galaxa-promethium*, a semi-radioactive element that not only has stable isotopes but whose elements can be harnessed to

HIS HIGHNESS THE DUKE

fuel long voyaging starships. Normally, only very trivial amounts of the element could be found naturally."

"Who are your people?"Aeron asked. She tried to hide her suspicion. Kendall expressed interest in the mine and knew a lot about fuel. If she wasn't interested in marriage like the other brides, then what was she doing here? Sure, Aeron wasn't there for marriage either, but what were the odds more than a couple brides had ulterior motives on the trip? Was Kendall a spy?

"They are called Haven, like me, Kendall Haven," Kendall said.

It wasn't exactly the answer Aeron had been looking for. She opened her mouth to ask more specifically about the woman's race, but the door slammed open, cutting her off. Bron stood, hair and clothes covered with dirt. His eyes glowed yellow, though his body carried little other evidence of a shift.

"What happened to you?" Aeron demanded, quickly standing. Relief flooded her and she hurried toward him. She didn't realize how scared she had been until that moment, looking at his dirty face.

"Spoken like a true wife," Alek muttered, stepping past his brother to move toward the table.

MICHELLE M. PILLOW

Aeron frowned at the man. Alek's return expression was unreadable, so she chose to not answer.

"It is nothing for you to be concerned over," Bron dismissed. He rubbed lightly at his wrists and she saw thick red marks on his flesh as if he'd been bound.

"Nothing to be concerned over?" Aeron repeated in disbelief. Was he serious? "How can you say that? You disappeared. There was no trace of you anywhere and then you come back, looking like you clawed your way out of a gravesite, and you say it's nothing to be concerned over? Are you daft?"

"Were you," he paused, "concerned about me?"

His Qurilixian accent rolled softly over her. A look of pleasure crept into his eyes, as the corner of his mouth lifted.

"Well, I…" Aeron mumbled. She wasn't sure when or how, but he had come closer. His heat radiated over her. Even though he smelled like the forest floor, she was drawn to him. She felt a strange sensation in her brain, as if he was inside her mind, whispering words she could not understand, urging her to say things she didn't know how to say.

"I doubt your wife would dishonor our family name with worry," Alek said loudly, reminding them that there were two other people in the cabin. "No woman would want a weak husband that hides behind her skirts."

"Dishonor?" Kendall asked loudly. "How is being worried about someone dishonorable?"

"You should trust the will of the gods, and in the strength of your man," Alek answered, as if it was a well known fact.

"So now it's a man thing?" Kendall asked. "I'm not sure I like your tone. Are you implying that women are weaker than men? That we should just sit back and let the men folk handle everything?"

Aeron's first instinct was to give the other couple privacy, but she didn't move. She wanted to hear the answer.

"Yes," Alek answered without hesitation.

"Yes?" Kendall repeated. "Did you actually just say that?"

Alek looked confused. He shot a hard glance at his brother.

Aeron turned to Bron. "Is that what you think? Men are to rule over women?"

"I would not say rule," Bron answered, his tone much more careful than Alek's had been. "But I do know women should never rule over men—save perhaps the queen over our people, or noblewomen over those beneath her station so long as it is done with benevolence. Between husband and wife there is a clear distinction. Do you not wish for a husband that can protect you and make you proud?"

"There can and should be compromise, but men who are guided too easily by women are not real men," Alek added. "Such a man could not protect you, provide for you, give you strong sons."

"And a woman's role in marriage is where? Cooking and having children?" Kendall demanded. If Alek had been a smart man, he would not have answered that question. Aeron almost cringed for him as he opened his mouth to reply. She would have felt sorry for him, if the two men weren't making her just as angry as Kendall appeared to be.

"Yes," Alek said. He did not relent. His eyes began to glow gold in the light.

Aeron closed her eyes briefly. This wasn't good. Was Alek an idiot?

"I see," Kendall spat. "It's a wonder your gods bothered to give us women brains at all when really all we needed were bellies to hold children and hands to serve our master husbands."

"I did not say—" Alek began.

"Do not say another word," Kendall warned, lifting her hand toward his face. "I have had it with men in my life trying to tell me what to do. We had

HIS HIGHNESS THE DUKE

an arrangement, if you recall, and I expect you to keep to it."

Aeron, understanding Kendall's anger, and feeling it to a lesser degree, turned to Bron. "You believe as your brother does?"

Bron nodded. He honestly looked confused, as if he couldn't understand what had made the women so upset. "I think you would want a strong husband. Why would you wish for a man who cowers behind your skirts and who drops his sword at the first sign of trouble? Such a man is not a man. Such a man would not bring honor to his family. Such a man cannot protect his family."

Her mind swam with thoughts, taking a dramatic turn. "Why would we need protection by sword?"

"The Var," Bron stated. "Our enemy. Many believe there will be another war soon. If there is, we will be expected to lead our men to battle."

"Sword battle?" Aeron swallowed. She had known this place was primitive, but it never occurred to her that the minor skirmishes referred to in the Galaxy Brides' uploads were code for all out hack and slash war.

"Yes. The sword is an honorable weapon." Bron nodded, as if such thing was common knowledge in the galaxies.

"You defend yourselves with swords?" Aeron

MICHELLE M. PILLOW

shook her head. They would not stand a chance against the Tyoe.

"It is the way of battle," Bron said.

"Kendall!" Alek ordered behind them. Aeron turned just in time to see Kendall storm out of the front door. "Kendall, the forest may not be safe. I need you to stay inside while we—Kendall!"

Aeron jolted as Alek marched past her to go after his wife. When she was alone with Bron, she took a step back.

"I do not understand your look of displeasure," Bron said.

"I'm just worried about—" She stopped herself, realizing what she was saying. Aeron turned her gaze from the front door where Alek disappeared to where she now stood alone with Bron.

"Do you need me to prove my worth to you?" Bron stiffened.

"No. I have no wish to see you go into battle with your sword drawn." Aeron frowned. "Should we go after them? If there is a threat in the forest—"

"Should I be insulted that you doubt not only my abilities but those of my brother?" Bron's expression had become tight and his eyes hard. "I have never had my name so insulted, but to hear such things from a wife!"

"I am not your wife," Aeron shouted back,

150

surprising herself with the forcefulness of it. Maybe it was a combination of the worry she'd felt when he was gone—a worry she was apparently not supposed to feel. Maybe it was the long days journeying over alien terrain with a ceffyl. Maybe it was the fact that she was torn between telling him about the possible attack and insisting on talking directly to the king. These people would not survive an air raid. Swords would do nothing against a fighter ship zipping across the sky. She took a deep breath. "Are you sure it was these Vars who attacked you?"

"I do not wish to discuss the Var," he snapped. "We must settle this matter of you being my wife."

"There is nothing to settle." Aeron couldn't keep looking at him. His anger frightened her and his presence rekindled her desires. The emotions contradicted each other. She turned her back on him and made it to the table where the uneaten food had gotten cold.

"Why are you resisting this marriage?" he asked. "Why can't you accept what we have?"

"I accept what we have done." She couldn't think about the fact that she was dying because of it. She wished she could blame him, but she had been the one to mindlessly take him while he was tied to the bed. She had no one to blame but herself. "I cannot mislead you into thinking I accept a marriage. In the long term, we would not work. We barely work now."

"You have not given us a chance to work."

"I know I will not be satisfied spending the rest of my days cooking and having babies." She looked at the plates of food she had made. She did enjoy making the food, but it was because it was not expected of her. She didn't want to be forced into such housewife duties. Her existence might be boring to some, but it was hers. She liked listening in on secrets and helping people with her thorough attention to details.

"Perhaps Alek stated the position too bluntly. These things you say are not all life with me will be. I offer much more than cooking and babies. And if you do not wish to cook, then I will find someone who will. Honor is not just about the duties we perform but in the way we act every day."

"What happened to you? You're covered in dirt." She didn't want to talk about marriage and children.

"I was captured in the forest. I awoke beneath the ground. I was working on freeing myself when Alek found me." He said the words so matter of factly, as if such a thing was a normal occurrence.

Aeron shivered. "You didn't see who took you?"

"No."

"Then how do you know it was the Var?"

HIS HIGHNESS THE DUKE

Aeron didn't look at him but felt him moving behind her. She focused on him, sensing where he was in the room.

"Who else would it be but our ancient enemy?"

"Is that how the Var normally fight?" Aeron touched the edge of the trencher, tracing it as she pushed the plate away from her.

"No. Not usually. This is very far north. Normally they stay south of the borderlands. If you must know, it is very unlike them to take an enemy without facing them. Perhaps they were coming back to deal with me. As a nobleman, they could have felt my capture was worth the risk of our mountain terrain. If I had not allowed myself to be distracted by your presence, I would not have been taken."

She ignored the last comment. There was no way she would take the blame for it.

"You said you were related to the king and that you are a nobleman here?" Aeron finally forced herself to look at him. Her eyes met his. He'd come closer, but not close enough to touch. She was glad for the distance. Bron nodded that he was both. "I work as a civilian contracted analyst for the Federation Military. The reason I was on the Galaxy Brides' ship was to come here to warn you."

"We are not part of the Federation Alliance. Why would the Federation send you?" He crossed

153

his arms over his chest. She hated the look on his face—the suspicion and unspoken accusations.

"No, it's not like that. The Federation didn't send me. They didn't give me permission to come. I'm a civilian and if this was sanctioned, they would have sent a trained operative to make contact with you. That is why I had to get a ride on the Galaxy Brides' ship." She swallowed nervously, wishing he would take his steady gaze off her. She felt like a soldier about to be interrogated by a superior officer. Her words were soft and nervous. "I hope I'm doing the right thing."

"Tell me." It was an order. There was no mistaking the tone.

"As far as I understand it, the Federation has little interest in your planet or your people, but for one thing."

"Our mining operations," he concluded.

Aeron nodded. "They have you labeled as a primitive planet with no military or scientific value other than the ore. And, since you mine the ore, doing the manual labor yourselves, they see no reason to interfere with your world."

"And that is the way we prefer it," Bron said.

She ignored his irritated injections, as she continued, "About five months ago, I intercepted some data. When I reported it to my superiors, they refuscd to get involved because you are not part of

HIS HIGHNESS THE DUKE

the alliance. So long as they get the ore, they said they would be keeping their hands clean of the whole situation. I was ordered to stop listening to the wavelength and to ignore all further information coming from that sector."

"What did you hear?"

"I hope I'm doing the right thing."

"What did you hear, Aeron?" he repeated, more insistent.

"The Federation insisted I do not get involved, but please understand I couldn't just say nothing and let something happen. I had to warn you."

"Aeron, tell me."

"A race of aliens called the Tyoe plan to attack your planet and set up a mining colony."

"I have not heard of these Tyoe. Why would they wish to attack us?"

"They're technologically advanced," she said. "They have mining bases all over the galaxy. It is my belief that the Federation thinks they're coming here might have great benefit as their technology could mine the ore faster than," she paused, not wanting to insult him, "than your older techniques."

"How do you know what our techniques are? We do not share them with outsiders."

"Well, I don't, I'm just saying with the way you live, it would be natural to assume you don't have the same kind of technology a race like the Tyoe would have."

He considered her words for a long moment. Then, carefully, he reasoned, "You could have forwarded a transmission to tell us this. Your being here can only mean the gods compelled you to come to me. There is a reason you were the one to hear the transmission. There is a reason you came to this planet. We were meant to find each other."

Was this man completely daft? Or did he just have marriage on the brain? "The Federation monitors my communications and it was doubtful, should I even find a secure line to tell you, that you would listen to a complete stranger on the wavelengths. I had to come."

"Did you try to contact us over the wavelengths?"

"Well, no, but—"

"You were compelled to come here. The gods willed it."

"No, you're not listening. I was compelled, yes, but not to be a wife. You don't understand. I have my reasons for having to warn you and they have nothing to do with marriage."

"Then tell me. What other reasons have you?"

"It's…" Aeron thought of her dead family, of her destroyed home world. She didn't like talking

HIS HIGHNESS THE DUKE

about it. Her reasons had no bearing on the outcome of her information. "It's personal."

"Why are you fighting this?" Frustration seeped out of him.

"Why are you refusing to listen? What I'm telling you is a real danger to your people and your planet, but all you want to talk about is marriage and…" Aeron frowned. "Perhaps I was mistaken. You are not the person I need to discuss this with. I need to speak to the king, or whoever is in charge of the mines. Who is in charge of the mines?"

"My brother, Mirek."

"Take me to Mirek," she said. "If you don't, I will find him myself."

"I assure you I heard everything you said and will do what must be done to ensure the safety of my people. That duty does not negate the fact that we need to get this marriage settled. In fact, settling this marriage is the first step in my doing anything about this attack. I am under direct orders from the king to make this marriage right before I leave this cabin. The sooner we do that, the sooner I can look into this Tyoe matter."

"That is blackmail."

"This is reality."

"So either I agree to stay married to you and you let me leave this cabin to warn your people of

157

possible annihilation, or I deny the marriage and watch a planet die?"

"Possibly die," he corrected.

"Possibly die," she repeated. "Blackmail."

"Reality."

"It is blackmail." She shook her head. "Do you really want a marriage based on blackmail? You don't know me. You don't know anything about me, or my people."

You don't know that I'm dying because of what we did. You don't know how hard it was for me to come here. You don't know what you're asking of me.

"I know enough. The gods decreed it. You are my wife and I your husband. We are meant to be."

Aeron closed her eyes, unable to keep looking at him. He seemed so earnest, so sure, but he said nothing of feelings, of his desire for her, or of love growing in time—not that she had that much time left. This was about duty, about some perceived supernatural force that commanded they be together. Yes, she felt a connection to him. She felt the physical pull to be next to him, to touch him and kiss him. She felt him like she had never felt any man. But was that fate? Or was it lust for the one man she had sex with?

"Know that I only say yes because you give me no choice." She remembered every second of her planet being destroyed, every piece of spinning rock, every flaming arc, every silent moment. She imagined there were screams on the surface, but in the spaceship, looking on from the window, feeling the pleasure of homecoming drain into disbelief and despair, it had been quiet. With her own death suddenly very near, she knew this might be her last chance to do something meaningful with it. She had nowhere else to go. The Federation would be furious with her. Perhaps this was her fate. It didn't stop her from resenting the way her marriage came about, or his high-handed blackmail disguised as decrees. "I request we leave as soon as possible."

Bron couldn't move. Aeron refused to look at him, but he couldn't stop staring at her. A tear slid from her eye, down her cheek. The lonely trail hurt him worse than anything she could have said at that moment. Her voice stayed steady, but that one tear gave so much away.

She did not want to be with him. He should let her go. How could he demand she stay with him as a wife? How could he keep her when she was miserable at the very idea? How could he let her go? She was his one chance at happiness. Surely she would come to love him, at least care for him.

He would be a good husband. He would do everything required of him and more.

He couldn't let her go. No matter if it would be the right thing to do, he just couldn't bring himself to release her from her vows. He'd bonded to her. For him, there would never be another woman. It was the way of his kind.

He lifted his hand, intent on going after her as she moved toward the back sleeping chamber, but he saw the dirt on his fingers. How could he have forgotten his ordeal? Hunger suddenly bit at his stomach and he eyed the untouched trencher of food. He had the Var to worry about, and apparently the Tyoe. Despite her misgivings, he was glad Aeron had seen reason and agreed to their marriage. He would inform Alek and then he would leave in the morning to see the king. Tonight he would eat, bathe, and... Bron looked to where his wife had disappeared down the hall. And gods willing he would find a way to comfort his wife.

9

Bron hesitated outside the sleeping chamber door, listening to the sounds coming from within. He wasn't afraid to face his wife, just his wife's tears. What did he know about comforting women, especially when he was the cause of her pain? He'd rather face a thousand swords than a woman's tears.

He didn't hear the sound of crying and decided it was safe to enter. She lay on the bed, her back to him. A wave of sadness washed over him. Already they were connecting, at least they were on his end. Soon he would be able to feel her emotions as if they were his. It was all part of the process. In fact, she might even start hearing his call inside her mind, if she opened herself up to what they could be to each other.

Bron stood, helplessly not knowing what to say to comfort her. He'd always thought if he stayed honest and did his duty then everything would work out. Well, he was doing his duty, the best he could, and she was still upset.

"I did not wish to upset you, my lady," he said quietly. Apologizing wasn't exactly a Draig trait. He had no practice at it.

"You have not upset me." The sound was muffled by the bedding. She didn't move to look at him.

"I think we both know that is not necessarily accurate."

"It was not you that upset me," she said. "You have your beliefs. I am on your planet. I must respect that your culture is different than mine and that I am in your territory and the mercy of your generosity."

"I do not wish for you to fear me." He didn't move. He wanted to go to her, to touch her. Actually, he wanted to stop talking altogether and just make love to her. Physical, he could handle. He was a man, a warrior. He was more comfortable with action over speaking of feelings. "You should not feel as if you are at my mercy."

She turned to look at him, her eyes dry and her expression steady. He let loose a small breath of relief. He'd felt her sadness and thought she might

HIS HIGHNESS THE DUKE

be overcome with tears, her face wet from sobbing. He moved slowly, not wanting to ruin the delicate moment.

"I do not fear you," she said. The sound was soft, almost a whisper. "I fear what will happen to your planet if you do not prepare for the Tyoe. I fear that my coming here will be a failure. I cannot watch another," she paused, correcting herself, "I cannot watch your people be annihilated. And, on this subject, I fear there is something else I'm bound to mention. When I spoke to Kendall earlier, she seemed unsure of her staying married. There was something secretive in her tone. I cannot place it. I'm not one to begrudge a woman her secrets, I have enough of my own, but I am not convinced you should tell your brother of the Tyoe until you are sure of her reasons for being here. The odds that more than a couple women on the ship came here on the Galaxy Brides' ship for reasons other than marriage seems highly unlikely. If I am wrong about her, then I am sorry for it, but I would rather err on the side of caution."

"Our fate is in the hands of our gods. They sent Kendall to my brother just as they sent you here to warn us. When I speak of this to my brother, I will mention your concern, but I assure you we will not be overtaken so easily." He lifted his chin, prideful. The rest of the galaxy might not

MICHELLE M. PILLOW

see their technology, but it did not mean they were a backward people who could not defend themselves against an enemy. They merely chose to live simply, hiding their technology away. In fact, hidden near the palace, disguised as a mountain peak, the Draig kept a highly advanced communications and watch tower. They monitored the stars at all times.

"Right. Gods." She shook her head and turned her face away from him once more, settling into her original position on the bed. "Of course you would believe in their protection. You let them dictate everything else."

"You do not believe there is something greater than ourselves?"

"No. I do not believe," she whispered. He wondered if he was meant to actually hear the words since they were so soft. Louder, she added, "If you are so sure about this fate of yours, I would prefer you not mention my concern to your brother. There is no reason to insult the woman without proof."

Bron wasn't sure how to answer such an admission. Her lack of belief worried him. Instead, he changed the course of the conversation. "We leave in the morning for the palace. I will report what you have told me to my uncle. The king will ensure necessary precautions are made at the palace. Then

HIS HIGHNESS THE DUKE

we will speak to my brother, Mirek, about the mines."

"How can you do that?" Suddenly she sat up and looked at him. He frowned, confused by her meaning. "You were just kidnapped, buried alive, restrained by the looks of those marks on your wrist, and now you're here bathing and talking and planning trips like nothing happened. I had to face an empty mountain path on an alien planet with the ugliest creature alive and I'm still shaking from it." As if to prove her point, she lifted her hands toward him. They did tremble a little. "I don't think my heart has stopped racing. Your ordeal is presumably much worse than my part of it, and yet you act as if you are buried beneath the ground several times a year. What exactly goes on here? Should I expect to be abducted next?"

With each sentence her tone became more frantic. He rushed to the bed, crawling onto the mattress to take her hands and press them to his chest. "I will not allow anything to happen to you."

"But what about what happened to you? How can you act as if it was nothing? And don't lecture me on worrying again. I'll worry about whatever I wish and it has nothing to do with honor or duty but a chemical reaction inside a person's body. And I don't understand why you won't just tell me what happened to you. I woke up and you were gone. I was terrified. I know nothing about alien terrain and survival. I don't even frequent the virtual reality deck."

"I was not buried alive. I was held prisoner underground."

"You say that as if it is better." She tried to pull her hands away from him, but he held tighter. She seemed so small and delicate. He wanted nothing more than to protect her.

"I am well. It is done," he said, soothingly. Bron inched closer to her on the bed. He tried to feel inside her, past the sadness. Instantly, her breathing deepened and her eyes closed. It was as if she was trying to feel inside him as he felt her. Such a connection could not be undone. If they bonded completely, they would be able to read each other's feelings.

A sudden fear filled him and he drew himself back, closing his feelings off from her. If they bonded, she would be able to sense what he was feeling. She would find the shame of his insecurity, his desperation to please her, his fear of failing her and of losing her. He couldn't let her know. If she found out all that was inside him, she might leave him. He would be forced to feel the loss of her even more potently once the connection was formed.

Bron leaned closer to her. She looked so pretty with her wide eyes staring up at him and her lips

HIS HIGHNESS THE DUKE

parted just enough to let her breath pass. Desire filled him. He wanted her. She said she would stay. Were the gods pleased? Was his capture punishment enough? It didn't seem a steep enough price to pay. No price would be equal to her.

Her lips met his first, as if answering his unasked question. The sweet taste of her mouth erased all thoughts. She moaned softly against him. He couldn't help himself. He slid his tongue between her lips. A rush of pleasure coursed through them. He felt her intake of breath, her soft moan of approval. Right now, she did not seem to protest their union.

Bron took the delicate truce, well aware of how a wrong word could break the moment. He could not help the filtering of his emotions as he let her inside him. A fog worked its way over their senses, fading the outside world. The spell of her kiss pulled him closer. How could this woman not know the power she held over him? How could she not feel it? In that moment, in that kiss, Bron knew Aeron had the power to enslave him.

Aeron inched closer. Her hands ran up the length of his arms to rest on his shoulders. He pressed the small of her back, sliding her against him. They knelt on the bed. His arousal formed into her stomach, causing him to groan.

She pulled her mouth from his. "The door."

MICHELLE M. PILLOW

Bron tried to pull her back to his mouth.

She turned her head to the side and pushed at his chest. "You need to close the door. Your brother and Kendall are here."

He glanced over his shoulder. Bron thought he had closed it. Reluctant to let her go, he hesitated before finally moving off the bed to do as she bid. This time, he made sure the door latched shut before turning to her. Aeron crawled to the edge of the bed, still on her knees. She smiled at him, the look inviting. Whatever her reluctance to be married to him, it would seem it did not carry over into their bedroom.

This time when he went to her, he stood by the bed. He caressed her cheek, running the pad of his thumb across her beautiful lips. Aeron tugged at the hem of his tunic, easing it up over his head. He lifted his arms to help her as she undressed him. With his chest bare, she began to explore. He stood before her, letting her touch him however she wished. She traced the outline of his muscles. Bron did not know how he managed to stay calm. The delicate skating of her fingers was tickling torture, but when she leaned forward to kiss one of his nipples it was pure agony.

Bron's hands shot forward into her hair, keeping her mouth against his chest. His fingers tangled in the dark length. Her fingers danced

HIS HIGHNESS THE DUKE

along his waist, close to the waistband of his breeches. His stomach tensed as she neared his navel.

He lifted her by her head to his mouth and kissed her deeply, sliding his tongue against hers. All thoughts left him as he pulled at the gown she wore. The material hugged firmly to her skin and did not strip from her body as quickly as he would have liked. He was about to rip it when she leaned back and helped his efforts. She pulled the gown over her head and tossed it aside. Bron used the moment to push the loose-fitting pants from his hips.

She came to him, as eagerly as he went to her. Her hands cupped his face, caressing his cheeks as she drew his mouth tenderly to hers. Their naked bodies pressed together. The soft mounds of her breasts molded to his chest. His erection pressed tight to her stomach. The memory of their joining was all too fresh and his cock surged to repeat the act. He wanted her like he'd never wanted anything in his life.

With his feet planted on the floor next to the bed, he reached for her hips, lifting her by her buttocks. Her legs were forced open as he drew them forward to wrap around his waist. She sat on the edge of the bed, her ankles hooking around the backs of his legs. Her breasts rubbed intimately against him, the nipples hard points he could feel dragging against his flesh.

Bron growled, unable to contain his excitement. He held her hips tight, keeping her sex against his arousal. The wetness of her body moistened him. He shifted his weight so he could lay claim to her, angling her body back as he leaned forward. He braced his feet on the floor and his hands on the bed.

The tip of his erection found entrance into her body. He pushed slowly, enjoying the firm grip of her sex. Her thighs moved against his waist, tightening and releasing as if she tried to decide whether or not to allow him entrance. He pressed on, drawn to lay claim to his wife. The thought occurred to him that this should have been their first time. In many ways it felt like the first. They were both aware, unclouded by the call of the crystal, unhampered by the guilt.

Her dark hair spilled around her head on the bed. She clung to him, her thighs closing and opening, closing and opening, gripping and releasing his waist. He stroked her face, letting his fingers trail down the center of her chest. Grabbing the delicate mound of flesh, he massaged it as he urged himself deeper.

She arched her hips against him, finally opening her legs and allowing him full access to her

HIS HIGHNESS THE DUKE

body. He took it, delving forward to seat himself fully inside her. The firm clench of her pussy held his arousal tight. Her insides quivered around him.

Aeron made sweet, light noises of pleasure. The sounds were as delicate as she was. Bron withdrew only to slowly push forward. He kept the rhythm easy, enjoying the view of her breasts moving with his thrusts. He wanted it to last forever.

He kissed her, working his mouth against hers. His tongue mimicked the slow pumping of his hips. Staying inside her, Bron placed one knee on the bed and then the other. He moved her with his body so he could lie on top of her. Now that she was fully beneath him he began to thrust anew. The new position allowed him to go deeper, allowed his strokes to be longer. He pumped into her, the speed growing with each pass. Each agonizing glide of flesh was pure ecstasy.

"More," she whispered, meeting the movements of his body. "Give me more."

Watching her body was almost as wonderful as feeling it. Her legs wrapped his waist, forcing him harder into her. He gave her what she wanted. It was what he wanted, too. His finger found the sensitive nub guarding her sex. He encircled it with fast strokes as he pushed her onward, hammering his violent need into her slick core, leading her to her pleasure and pushing her over the trembling edge.

She closed her eyes. Her hands grabbed hold of his arms and squeezed tight. Her breath caught in her throat and she began to shake. Bron pumped faster. Her body seized hold of him as she came. The feel of her climax was too much. He growled as he joined her, liberating all the pent up frustration in one hot jet of release.

As he slowly came down from the height of pleasure, he pulled himself free of her. Staring deeply into her eyes, he stretched next to her on the bed. He pushed a strand of hair from her forehead. Bron didn't know what to say, so he stayed quiet. She didn't seem to mind the silence as she settled next to him. He slid an arm over her waist in possession and protection.

He closed his eyes and was content to listen to her breathe.

"How old are you?" she whispered. "The Galaxy Brides' uploads said your people lived for five hundred years."

"Worried that you are married to an old man?" He gave a soft laugh. Out of all the things he thought she might want to know about him that was not one of them.

"No," she answered, not moving. "If what the

upload says is true, you will live long past my death."

"Here, wives live as long as husbands," he answered. "Usually. Scientists believe that it has to do with the radiation from our sun. Spiritualists believe it is the will of the gods. I believe it is both."

"Usually," she repeated, sighing deeply, "but not always."

"You worry I will not keep you safe?" he asked. The words hurt, even as he was the one to lay voice to them. She really did not have much faith in his honor, or his abilities as a husband. How could he blame her? He should have stopped the joining on the wedding night. He should have been stronger. Bron knew the blame fell fully on his shoulders, regardless of the actual physical position they'd been in. The gods were not pleased with him.

"Sleep well," she whispered, refusing to answer him. "We have a long journey in the morning."

10

AERON WASN'T sure what to say as the ceffyls carried them toward the palace. Perhaps it was best she said nothing. Her eyes turned to the skies, wondering when the Tyoe might attack. She was unclear as to the attack timeline, but had gotten a sense that it wasn't in the too distant future. Then she looked around the landscape, to each hidden curve of path, to each tree and shrub. Were enemies hiding even now? Waiting to attack two unarmed travelers? Were these Var going to capture them on the ground? Were the Tyoe going to bury them alive?

She glanced at Bron who rode his own mount. They had left Alek and Kendall without a ceffyl, but the brothers had determined speed was a necessity. Bron had changed his clothing. Clearly a supply had been stored at the cabin for the men. He wore a clean green tunic with gold embroidered edges. The tunic was designed like a long shirt that hung to his knees and split at the sides, opening to reveal his thighs as he sat astride the fearsome beast. He'd given her a similar overtunic in blue to put over the undertunic she'd been given the morning after the ceremony. The only thing she could say about it was that at least it was clean.

Nothing about this planet felt safe. It was primitive. The people were primitive. She desperately wanted the safety of a spaceship with monitored life support systems and loud warning alarms if security was breached. She wanted her small metal room, food simulator, and laser decontaminator. She wanted air control systems that monitored for airborne viruses and… Viruses. She hadn't thought about that until now. Her fear grew. What if this primitive planet had primitive diseases that were attacking her on a biological level? Nothing was safe. Planetary attacks. Space attacks. Biological attacks. And she was—

"Aeron?"

Aeron jolted in alarm, letting go of a small scream. She grabbed her chest. Her heart beat hard in her chest as she looked at him.

"What is it? Do you hear something?" He tilted his head, listening. The question was laughable. As

HIS HIGHNESS THE DUKE

a shifter, his senses would be much more advanced than hers.

"I was—" She gave a self-depreciating shrug. In truth she was working herself into a fearful mess. "I was thinking."

Overthinking a situation wasn't a new problem for her. She would think about an issue until it was analyzed from every direction. If she wasn't careful, she would think herself into a nervous, certifiably insane wreck.

"About?" he prompted. Bron sounded hesitant to even ask. She couldn't blame him.

"I miss my quarters."

"You mean your home? On a ship?"

Home. No, she'd never really thought of her quarters as home. She supposed that was what it was, but in her mind home was a place that no longer existed.

"Tell me about it."

"I can't," she whispered.

"Because I do not have the Federation's permission or clearance? I assure you, I can be trusted. I am your husband. Your secrets are mine. However, if you gave your word before wc met, I will not ask you to dishonor yourself by breaking it. If you say you cannot tell me, I will believe and trust you."

"I can't because there is no home to speak of," she corrected. "I doubt the Federation cares if I tell

MICHELLE M. PILLOW

you which ship base I was assigned to. As for clearance, I've already broken protocol by coming here and telling you about the Tyoe. I was kidding myself to think I could go back there after doing this. I would be lucky if they just imprisoned me for treason."

"Then why take the risk?" he asked.

"The will of the gods, of course," she answered, trying not to smirk. He stiffened visibly. "Sorry. I was trying to lighten the mood."

He relaxed some.

"I have my reasons. Thank you for not prying into them." Her words purposefully cut off any inquiry. Thinking of it made her think of her sister. She wondered where Riona was. It wasn't like they were close, or that she knew where her sister was on most days, but she couldn't help but wonder what had happened to Riona after the ceremony.

He nodded and to her surprise he didn't push the subject. "Do you think you can handle a faster gait?"

Her backside was a bit sore, but the idea of getting to the palace faster did have merit. "Yes. I can ride faster."

Bron made a low noise and both beasts instantly picked up their pace. The sound of their hooves resounded over the countryside. Gritting her teeth, she held on to the center horn and gripped the beast with her legs. This was going to be a hellish day.

Aeron could not feel her butt or the backs of her legs. No, actually, it was worse than that. Her toes were tingling. Her fingers were numb from gripping the center horn. Her back was jarred and felt as if someone spent the last three hours throwing rocks into it. Her neck was stiff, her head pounded, and any energy she had to smile at the Draig soldiers had been left on the side of the pathway.

The path led them from the mountains and along a practice field of soldiers behind the royal palace. The shifter men, all of them burly and fierce, stared after her. A few smiled but most silently watched as if judging her. She had kept her eyes down, wishing she looked more presentable. Next to her, Bron looked handsome and regal. She looked like some piece of spacedrift he'd taken pity on.

Wrought iron gates lifted high over the entrance leading into the side of a large mountain. From the distance, the mountain looked like any other, but Aeron soon detected a palace entranceway camouflaged within the red stone. Wide domes allowed light inside the tunneled path of red rock. Then, entering a front door of thick oak, they came to a series of passageways.

Bron spoke to the guard in the gruff Draig language. She held back, trying not to draw notice to herself as they were let into the palace. Bron led the way through the passageways. The mountain castle was as picturesque as she would have expected a castle to be. It was clean and decorated with tasteful paintings and sculptures. Tapestries hung on the walls, alongside banners with the emblem of the royal dragon.

The main hall of the Draig palace had steep, arched ceilings with the center dome for light. According to Bron, the banners along the walls were of the royal family crest, one for each color of the family lines—purple for the king and queen, green for Prince Olek, red for Prince Zoran, blue-gray for Prince Ualan, and black for Prince Yusef. Each had the silver symbol of the dragon. Lines of tables reached across the floor for dining. The red stone floor was swept clean, and the hall was empty but for a couple servants. Upon seeing the new arrivals, they quickly left them alone.

"Aren't we going to get cleaned up first?" Aeron asked, looking at her male-cut long tunic smudged with travel dust.

"First we must greet the king and queen. It's

HIS HIGHNESS THE DUKE

customary." He followed her eyes downward. "You are beautiful."

"I see the affection of the crystal has not faded," Queen Mede interrupted as she entered the hall. She smiled at her nephew. "The king will be relieved to hear as much. He would have come to greet you but he is in a meeting."

The woman's smile appeared kind, but her eyes were sharp as she took in everything around her. She was immaculately dressed. A slight glint of liquid gold filtered in her gaze as she glanced over Aeron's clothing. Her smile fell some as she looked at her nephew. To Aeron's surprise, Bron actually looked sheepishly away from his aunt like a silently scolded child.

"You have come to assure us the match is well made?" the queen asked when no one spoke. "I admit I did not expect you to set it right so quickly, but I am pleased to have been proven wrong. It gives me much hope that my own sons will soon set right their marriages. You must excuse them from not coming to greet you."

"Is all well with the princes?" Bron asked.

Mede lifted her hand, refusing to elaborate more. "That story is still being written. I'll let your cousins' tell it once it is finished."

Bron nodded. Aeron found herself very curious as to what the queen meant by that. She

MICHELLE M. PILLOW

bit the inside of her lip, keeping herself from inquiring.

"I will have the guest wing prepared." The queen paused, glancing at Aeron's clothing. "The tailor is very busy with the princesses at this time, but I will send him to you. There is no reason he cannot tend to my niece as well." Mede sent a sharp look at her nephew.

"We thank you, my queen," Bron said. "There has been little time to see to such things at the cabin. In fact, I come back so quickly to speak to the king about an important planetary matter concerning the mines."

Mede stiffened. "He is in the office. You know the way."

Bron nodded. Aeron made a move to follow him from the hall. Mede caught her arm. "I will show you to the guest wing where you can relax."

"But…" Aeron tried to protest. She did not want to be left alone with the woman.

The queen was insistent. "Let the men deal with their business. I would have us get better acquainted."

By the time she turned to look after Bron, he'd disappeared. Aeron wished he would have waited for her. She wanted to hear what he said to the king, to make sure he told the man everything he needed to know. With little choice since the queen

HIS HIGHNESS THE DUKE

was looking at her expectantly, she dutifully moved to follow behind the woman.

Aeron didn't speak. What could she say? The woman was royalty, daunting in and of itself. She was also Bron's aunt. Suddenly, the full power of her new husband became all too real. He was related to royalty. Royalty! Even on a primitive planet it was an impressive position of power and responsibility.

Aeron glanced around the palace interior. Here it didn't feel so primitive. She saw hints of technology within the design. To the untrained eye it would be impossible to see, but she'd seen many technology specs in her works as an analyst. On occasion, it had been her job to analyze spec transmissions to make sure there were no hidden codes within them or anomalies in the blueprints.

The halls seemed endless, as if to purposefully create a maze to trap people inside. Finally stopping at a door, the queen gave a short command. The door slid open. Yes, the Draig had more technology than the outside of the place would let on. Inside was a home within the palace, an entire suite complete with kitchen and bathroom. It was one of the most stunning places she'd ever seen. The richness of it reminded her of the spa advertisement chips she collected but never traveled to.

Gray marble tiles contrasted the natural red of

the stone walls. Water cascaded down the entryway wall on both sides of the door. The gentle sound of water was somehow soothing. Light colored plants grew within the rock beds beneath the miniature waterfalls. The room was open, with a circular couch around a fire pit. Overhead a dome ceiling allowed light from outside to enter. The queen pushed a button, drawing back the oversize curtains to dim the light to a more comfortable level.

An opened doorway led to a kitchen. She recognized the appliances within it from her time at the cabin. Plants hung from the ceiling, connected by a yellowish vine with blue tinted leaves. The vine was strung about the room like a natural garland. An opened door revealed the bathroom close to the kitchen. Steam rolled from a tub, as water churned inside it. She wondered if it always ran, or if the bath had been somehow ordered because of Aeron's current unpresentable state.

"Riding ceffyls is not for everyone," the queen said, after giving her guest ample time to stare at her surroundings. "Or so I am told from women who come to this planet."

"That's right, you were born a shifter, I mean Draig," Aeron said, before she could stop herself.

"Yes," the queen smiled. "I am Draig." The woman let her eyes shift briefly. "It is good Bron

HIS HIGHNESS THE DUKE

told you of our gifts. Some men think to protect their wives and wait to tell them of it. As if being a dragon-shifter is something to be ashamed of."

"I think the rarity of the shifters in the universe is what can frighten people. It is fear of what is unknown," Aeron said softly. The queen kept looking at her like she should speak, but she was unsure what to say. "It seems a common enough theme amongst the alien cultures I've heard about.

Mede hummed thoughtfully.

"There is not much known in the universe about the Draig even in the Federation files or in Galaxy Brides' down—" Aeron continued, only to stop as the other woman perked up at the mention of the Federation.

"You come to us from the Federation?"

Aeron nodded. There was no point in hiding the fact since she'd come here to warn them. "Civilian analyst. It's why I came to your planet."

The queen moved toward the couch and sat. She gestured for Aeron to do the same. Aeron was slower to follow but did obey the silent command. After Aeron was settled, the woman said, "I thought you came to our planet to find love, not to analyze us."

"No."

"But you were on the Galaxy Brides' ship," the queen reasoned. She kept her gaze steady.

"It was the only ride we could find."

"We?" the queen prompted.

"I traveled with my sister. She knows how to get around the universe better than I do." Aeron tried to relax, but her back remained stiff. She looked at the fire pit. Its barren depths provided little to merit her full attention.

"I see. But you came here, met my nephew, and plans changed? Now you are Lady Aeron, the High Duchess of Draig, wife to the High Duke." The queen looked at her as if such a title should please her greatly.

Aeron didn't move. What could she say to that? She never really thought of herself as titled, of having power. The very notion of it caused her to shiver in worry.

"I see," the queen repeated, this time not as hopeful. "You have not decided to stay."

"I've been given little choice in the matter," Aeron corrected. She didn't want to speak badly of Bron to his family, but she also refused to lie.

"We all have a choice," the queen said. "I would ask you to consider yours very carefully, especially if you are thinking of leaving him. Surely you must already see how much Bron cares for you. It's obvious how deeply he feels."

Obvious? At that, Aeron's eyes shot up to meet the queen's. "You mean because his crystal glowed?

HIS HIGHNESS THE DUKE

That has to be a chemical reaction, some kind of biological indicator. I don't think it means love."

Queen Mede pushed forward from her seat, leaning toward Aeron. "I do not know how it works, or why. I don't question it because I know it does work. Qurilixian men, and we rare females, are given a crystal when we are born. It is our guiding light. When you were paired by the crystal, your lives became joined in such a way that can never be undone, not that I can imagine wanting to undo such a wonderful gift. You exchanged part of your souls. By crushing the crystal, you assured that the exchange would never be reversed. In a way, you are now his guiding light."

Aeron frowned. The woman seemed so sure of her words. "You said Qurilixian men. All Qurilixian men? The entire planet does this?"

"The Draig," Mede clarified. "Yes, all Draig. I do not consider the Var to be true men. They are our enemy and their ways very different from ours."

Aeron merely nodded.

"Do you understand what I am telling you, Lady Aeron? Do you know what breaking his crystal means for Bron?" the Queen asked.

Aeron shook her head in denial. She listened intently to every word.

"It means he put his every chance at happiness

on you. He gave his life to you, part of himself. There will never be anyone else for him as long as he lives."

Aeron felt tears entering her eyes. As long as he lived? That was hundreds of years more. Her life was severely shortened because of their physical joining. "And what if I do not live?"

"Then it will be a very sad affair. There will be no other in his bed or his heart. There simply can't be." The queen smiled kindly. Aeron found she liked the woman, even if she was a little bit intimidated by her power—both regal and physical. "It is why he will do everything he can to protect you. I know my nephews. They are like my sons. They can be overbearing and impossible at times. They will spin you in circles with their ways until you want to hit them over the head with the nearest rock. I can relate. I have thrown a few rocks at my husband. I may be Draig, but that only makes my situation worse. My husband treats me like a rare flower that needs constant guarding. In truth, shifted, I can hold my own against him."

Aeron swallowed nervously, trying to process all she was told. "I can't shift. I can't really do anything special."

Mede chuckled. "That is not true. You can love your husband and honor him. There is much to be said about that. All the grand schemes in the

HIS HIGHNESS THE DUKE

universe pale in comparison to love and family. All jobs mean nothing when put up against being a mother and wife and partner. That is not to say you cannot work if you so choose, but there is something very noble to also walking a simple path. I am queen. I rule half a planet. I have power and respect. I negotiate and entertain alien races, and yet if you ask me, do you know what I'd tell you my most important roles are?"

"Wife and mother," Aeron supplied.

The queen nodded. "Yes, family."

"Is it too late to stop the process? Can I find Bron another crystal?" Aeron knew Bron had explained some of this to her, but the queen had a way of explaining it that Bron did not. Her husband made it sound like a command that she stay with him, all dependent on duty and honor and tradition and fate.

"I have seen the way he looks at you. It is far too late for him. Whether he realizes the full connection or not, he *has* given you his life. He has shortened his days to extend yours so your fates could remain entwined. If you were to choose to leave him, he would be alone for the rest of his life. If you die, he will be alone. Without the aid of our blue sun, your life would play out like normal, maybe extended a few more years than usual. When he took you to his tent, it was his choice.

When you stayed, that was yours. You are all he will ever have. So, please, I beg you for the sake of my nephew and my family, consider your future very carefully. I see you thinking of going, of denying the marriage. I am sure Bron thinks you mean to stay. He could not, would not, have brought you back to the palace otherwise—not after the king ordered him to stay at the cabin until your marriage was made right."

Aeron couldn't deny it. She did think of leaving, not because she didn't care, but because she was scared of caring. The last home world she'd had exploded. Could she really accept a new one knowing what she did about the Tyoe? It seemed a choice destined for heartache and pain.

"How is all this possible? It can't just be the radiation," Aeron tried to reason. If it was true, when she died Bron would be alone. Was giving his years to her enough to counteract her lineage? She was scarcely able to believe as much.

"Why question it? You feel him, don't you? You have started to feel what he is feeling. And he feels what you are feeling. If you are discontent, he will feel it. It will distract him. If you are happy, he will smile more and not know why."

"If not love, then he could have companionship, at least, couldn't he?"

The Queen merely laughed, not shying away

HIS HIGHNESS THE DUKE

from the revealing question. "You are curious, aren't you? In the past, the boys have occasionally left our planet for ambassador duties. And, distasteful as it sounds, there are several roving bands of women with loose morals who make scheduled stops for the warriors. They are men after all. But that is all in the past. Such are the pursuits of unmarried men, a mere means to idle away the time until fate chooses their future. Once mated, they do not go back to such things. He couldn't if he wanted to. You would know right away. Besides, if he wanted to, you would know that, too. He doesn't desire anyone else, rest assured."

Aeron wasn't sure how to respond. She hadn't been asking about Bron's sex life, but the idea gave her much pleasure.

"I have given you much to think about. I love my family, but men are men and they sometimes forget that not everyone thinks as they do. I find it best to command information from them, if they are being evasive." Mede laughed. "I can see by your expression that evasiveness has been an issue. Those men and their secrets. Do they really believe they can keep them from their wives?" The queen stood and crossed the distance to Aeron. She cupped her cheek gently. "You have so much power, little niece, as do all women. Your husband will act like he is in charge, like he is protecting you and your honor. Let him think that, for in truth, you hold all the power in your marriage. If you accept him, he will give everything he is and everything he has to please you. Use that power well…"

Aeron nodded.

"…or I will have to hunt you down."

Aeron nodded again, looking for a sign the woman was joking. She wasn't.

"Good." The queen removed her hand and turned toward the bathroom. "I will leave you to bathe. We are about the same size, I think, so I will have some of my gowns brought to you."

"I can't possibly accept—" Aeron stood in protest.

"You cannot possibly walk around the palace dressed as you are," the queen corrected. "It is understandable after a journey, but not after you have been given our hospitality."

Aeron nodded. "I don't wish to embarrass anyone."

Let alone myself, she added silently.

"Then it is settled. You should find everything you need in these chambers." Medc gestured toward the bathroom. "Bron will join you when he's finished his business with the king."

HIS HIGHNESS THE DUKE

"Do you trust your wife?" King Llyr watched his nephew from behind his desk in the royal offices.

"Yes," Bron said without hesitation. He glanced from the fireplace to look over his shoulder at the king. "I would stake my word to hers."

"Then that is all I need to know." The king nodded, taking Bron at his word without hesitation.

Bron moved from where he had been staring into the fire. He walked with a natural grace to take his place before the king's desk. There were several documents in front of the man, including a very large stack of parchment contracts.

"This is not the most welcome news," the king said wearily, watching Bron with shaded eyes. "I have my hands full with the Var threat. They grow overbold as of late. This last batch of brides seems intent on being obstinate. None of the royal marriages are settled. I would cancel next year's shipment of potential brides until we can look into why this many are unsettled, but then I would have a riot on my hands with the men. Several of the soldiers will be ready to join the bachelors, and we will have a record number of men in attendance within the next five years. It would seem on the surface the royal and noble marriages have given the men hope. We have looked for years for another way to bring brides to our planet. Short of finding the legendary portals our ancestors were said to have buried beneath the earth, so that we may once again kidnap brides like savages, I have no alternative to Galaxy Brides."

Bron didn't answer. What could he say?

The king sighed. "All this and now I have to worry about a potential space attack by a race of aliens I have never heard of."

"Mirek will look into it and we will submit a report with our findings." Bron thought of his wife and wondered what she and the queen were discussing. He knew his aunt could be possessive of family and hoped Aeron didn't express any discontentment to the woman. The queen wouldn't hurt Aeron, but she wouldn't hesitate to put her into punishment.

"I will speak to Zoran and have him pick up the men's training. They will be sharp and ready. For now, we will tell them that it is because of the Var threat, which is not a lie. I do not want the men distracted by looking up to the skies for a possible threat when the Var are a very real one on this planet." The king glanced at the ceiling, as if he could see through the stone to the universe beyond.

"Let them try to take our mines," Bron said. "My brothers and I will be ready."

The king gave a small laugh, as if part of him welcomed the space battle. "I trust that you will. I

HIS HIGHNESS THE DUKE

will leave this matter to you. Speak to command in the communications tower, but no one else. Jorne is posted there. He's discreet. If an unauthorized ship comes close, we will be ready."

"I will before we leave."

"Your brothers should be home by now."

"All but Alek. I left him at the cabin."

"Of course." The king nodded. "Your rescue. It was very lucky your bride had the presence of mind to come toward the palace."

"Yes. It was." Bron didn't mention the fact his bride had probably done so out of fear rather than planning, but the bravest acts were those done in spite of fear. For that, he took much pride in his wife's actions.

"Your capture, though uncertain of origin, is very suspect. It does not sound like the Var to leave you in a pit to rot, but we cannot rule them out. I don't expect a cat-shifter to fight with honor. As I said, they grow restless and bold. I fear King Attor will soon lead an attack on the palace. I've heard rumors he was at the bridal festival, though nothing substantiated by anything more than men too far into their cups to be sure."

"My soldiers are ready, and the miners will defend their homes," Bron assured him. "I'll ensure the unused shafts are hidden and will double the guards on the others."

"Send reports," the king said. "And perhaps it is time we prepared the communication devices between the cabin and the palace. I'll order a technician to see to it."

"We haven't used them for nearly thirty years," Bron said. "Can they even be repaired? I think we used some of the parts to repair the link between my home and the palace about ten years back."

"Has it been so long?" The king shook his head. "It is no surprise. Who wishes to be disturbed by duty when hunting? It will be a shame to lose the solitude, but I will repair them nonetheless. We cannot be out of communication should there be an attack. Let's just hope the Var and these Tyoe don't take it to mind to attack the same day."

"I will have the system at my home checked as well." Bron had maintained the main communication line between his home and the palace, but the others had fallen to neglect from little use. Most news could be delivered in person and repairing the communication devices through the mountain ranges was no easy task. Satellite transmissions could be listened to, so they had to use ground methods.

"If we are lucky, one of you will have married a communication expert." The king smiled to himself, hopeful.

"I will ask Aeron. Perhaps she knows something

HIS HIGHNESS THE DUKE

about it. She was a communication analyst for the Federation. It is how she came about this news of a threat."

"A communication expert? See, the gods have a plan." The king grinned. "There is a reason Lady Aeron came to you."

At that Bron couldn't help but smile.

"If the attack proves true, we owe your wife a great deal. I will be sure to throw a banquet in her honor in a few years, once all these unruly marriages are settled and the princesses are well established."

In their world, a few years were nothing when compared to a lifetime of hundreds. Bron nodded. "My family would be honored by such generosity."

The king stood, wryly answering, "Generosity nothing. My wife enjoys entertaining and will love the excuse to get you boys here to the palace. Do not be surprised if she uses your brides to lure you here more often. We do not see enough of you."

"You have but to ask it and we will come," Bron said.

"Do not say as much to my wife. She will build you all wings and will never let you leave. She loves you like you are her own sons."

"If that is true," Bron said as he followed his uncle to the royal office's door, "then she will surely grow tired of all of us underfoot. I have heard her

197

scold her own sons, threatening to move them out to the mountains with their cousins."

"That was before they gave her daughters," the king corrected. "Now she is content. At least for the next twenty years. It is a small reprieve from her nagging, but I will take it." The king might have sounded serious, but Bron knew well the man adored his wife. He would be lost without her, as they all would. Mede was Llyr's universe, his very reason for being. There was no shame in it, only honor and love.

"Speaking of wives, I must find mine. We will not overstay our welcome this time. I should find Mirek and make sure the necessary precautions are underway."

"Stay one night. Morning will come fast enough and your mounts will be rested by then. If you leave any faster, it will cause speculation amongst the servants. You are welcome to dine in the hall, though I imagine newly married couples have little use for hall dining." The king held up his hand. "No. Before you refuse, I will simply decree that you dine in the guest chambers and work on producing some heirs the queen can spoil."

"Just the queen?" Bron quirked a brow.

"Perhaps I may be moved by generosity if children were produced in the family line," Llyr said, keeping his face blank. To a stranger the man

HIS HIGHNESS THE DUKE

would appear hard, but to family they all knew better.

"Yes," Bron mused. "Like the secret supply of miniature swords, shields, armor, and spears you ordered commissioned after last year's ceremony when it was decided your sons would attend?"

The king looked surprised.

"The blacksmith you hired works near my home. The royal insignia gave you away." Bron grinned. "Though ordering eighty-eight pairs? Do your sons know of your plans for a large family?"

"I do not know what you're talking about." The king pretended to rearrange papers on his desk. "Besides, it is only twenty-two grandsons per son. Half that when you count you boys. Not so excessive especially when you take into account the hundreds of childbearing years."

"Your secret is safe with me, your majesty." Bron laughed. "Though you must let me be there when you inform the new princesses they will be having twenty-two children... if only to help you escape the angry female mob that ensues."

11

"Do you like children?"

Aeron blinked her tired eyes open. She hadn't heard Bron enter the bathing room. She followed her first instinct to cover her chest with her arms. Since he had already seen her without clothes, it seemed like a foolish gesture. Still, she didn't move them to reveal her naked body in the bathwater.

The room was crafted out of the red stone of the mountain. The large tub had been carved into the stone floor with steps that led down into its depths. Natural spring water bubbled up from below only to be circulated and filtered so that the bathwater was always hot and clean. The bubbling pressure against her lower back felt too nice and she'd been reluctant to get out, even as her cheeks had turned bright red and sweat adhered her bangs

MICHELLE M. PILLOW

to her forehead. Servants had brought a tray of food and her full stomach combined with heat made her sleepy.

There was the normal primitive toilet and sink, as was to be expected on such a simplistic world, and a vanity counter that curved around the circular walls with a long mirror over it. Beneath the countertop were numerous cabinets, some with drying linens and others with toiletries. With a turn of a knob, the outside light directed throughout holes in the ceiling would dim and brighten.

"Do I like…?" she repeated slowly, trying to focus her thoughts. Bron looked handsome. His chest was naked and he was working on unfastening his pants. He appeared completely unconcerned by the fact she watched him undress.

"Like children," he said.

"I don't know any children." Aeron's hands relaxed some as her elbows slid back into the bathwater. She still hid herself from him. "What did the king say? Have the Tyoe made contact?"

"The king has ordered me take care of the matter. No, the Tyoe have not made contact." Bron moved to the bath. His eyes moved down to where her hands hid her breasts from view. "Do you want children?"

"I never considered it." It was the truth. Well, until the queen had mentioned family to her earlier,

HIS HIGHNESS THE DUKE

she hadn't really stopped to consider it. With her condition, it was not like she would be around to watch those children grow into later adulthood. Could she really do something like that to a child? She remembered all too well being without her parents, her people. It hadn't been a factor on her home world because parents would have children, who in turn would have children at the appropriate time and the cycle of life evened itself out. Now that she'd started her own biological clock, she didn't know what to think. Would they inherit her traits, or Bron's? Either way, she didn't have hundreds of years to be there for them. Perhaps her family line should die with her and Riona. What did she know about motherhood? She could barely fathom staying on world as a wife. Regardless, she was too tired to think about it at the moment. There was a more pressing matter. "So the king, he is taking the threat seriously?"

Bron stepped into the bath and slowly lowered his body in the center of the tub. She moved her legs to allow him access while staying next to the edge.

"Of course he is taking the threat on our people serious," Bron stated.

"What will we do?" Aeron hurriedly continued the conversation before he could switch it again.

"We?"

"You said the king put us in charge of the matter. What are we going to do first?"

"Us?" Bron shook his head. "No, he put me in charge of the matter. I will deal with it."

Aeron's hands dropped completely as she forgot to hide herself. She frowned at him. Coldly, she answered, "I see."

"Good." He began to reach for her. The man actually had the audacity to try and smile at her.

Aeron pulled back. "There is only room for one in here." Standing, she stepped out of the bath. "I'll leave you alone."

"But…" He stood in the bath. She witnessed the full length of his erection.

Aeron forced a dispassionate glance down his body. Wryly, she answered, "I'm sure you can deal with it." She walked out of the bathroom, naked and wet, and really not caring. Oh, but she was mad! Her hands shook with the force of it. The insufferable man was lucky she didn't try to drown that smug look off his face. If he wanted to act all high-handed, then he could do it on his own. She wasn't going to spend the rest of her short life being dismissed and treated like a servant.

She turned to look at the bathroom, half tempted to storm back in there and start throwing things at him. A shiver ran along her spine, spreading over her arms and legs. She should have grabbed one of the drying linens, but it was too late to go back and get one. Ignoring the kitchen, she went toward a narrow door hidden in the corner. It led to a bedroom, which she had explored earlier after the queen left her alone. The fur-covered bed was large and round with a pile of pillows in the center. A chill again worked over her damp flesh. Without thought, she whipped back the fur covers and crawled into bed. Grabbing a couple pillows, she tucked them around her body and under her head. The instant warmth invaded her body and she sighed in comfort, forcing herself to relax. Anger would do her no good. She needed to be rested and rational. The curtains overhead were drawn so the room was dim. She closed her eyes. The king was informed. Her mission was done. For the moment, she felt like she could finally rest.

Bron stared down at his erection in disbelief. She had left him to deal with it on his own. Such a thing wasn't unheard of. He could well handle his own physical needs. By all that was sacred, he'd taken care of such needs his entire adult life. That wasn't the point. He was married now.

Sex was the one thing they seemed to do well together. It was the one thing they had always

MICHELLE M. PILLOW

silently agreed on. How could she walk away from that? It was the one thread between them that gave him hope of a future, of a marriage, of a life. What happened? She had looked at him as if she didn't want him. She had left him to handle it himself.

Bron absently grabbed his arousal as he sat in the bath. He pumped it a few times, but the passion he'd felt moments before now made the gesture empty and disinteresting. Not bothering to finish, he dropped his hand and leaned against the edge of the hot bath. The churning water didn't feel as good as it should have. He watched the door, willing her to come back to him. She didn't.

If she lost her passion for him, then what would they have left?

Perhaps he should not have mentioned children.

Bron closed his eyes unable to concentrate. His body was tight with unreleased desire. With an irritated growl, he took himself in hand and began stroking. The angry tugs were hardly what he'd call pleasurable, more functional. His release came more as a relief of pressure than anything else. Then, grabbing liquid soap, he began lathering his skin.

Sacred stars, what did Aeron want from him? He couldn't understand her. She wanted to warn the king about the alien threat. He did that. She wanted the Tyoe situation dealt with. He was dealing with it. So why the sudden chilliness toward him?

Bron scrubbed his body harder. Talons grew from his nail beds in his frustration and he scratched himself. Small trickles of blood ran down his forearm into the water. So much for a relaxing afternoon with his wife. Ignoring the wound, he kept scrubbing. If the gods were still punishing him for the wedding night, they were doing a very fine job of it. Being married to Aeron was torture, almost as torturous as the idea of not having her at all.

"Accursed woman," he hissed under his breath. "What is it you want from me?"

AERON YAWNED, stretching her hands over her head. She looked up at the ceiling, automatically trying to discern how late in the evening it was. Her body was relaxed and her mind sleep-hazed, but the constant daylight on the planet made it hard to tell night from day. The light seemed less forceful than when she'd gone to bed, but she'd been so irritated with Bron she hadn't really been concentrating on the light and time.

Blinking, she was almost disappointed to see he

wasn't in the bed next to her. Ok, so she had dismissed him rather quickly. Well, he *had* been acting like an overbearing suctionite.

Throwing the covers off her body, she felt the chill of the room's air. It wasn't uncomfortable, just cooler than the warm cocoon of blankets she'd been enjoying. She tried to run her fingers through her hair, but the locks had dried into a tangled mess as she slept. With her vision adjusted to the darkened room, she looked around, able to see more clearly than before. A chair sat in the corner next to a narrow, wood-carved table. On the table were a neatly stacked pile of clothes. She went to them, looking for something to wear.

The queen had been most generous in her offer to give Aeron clothing. The richly made pile of dresses was almost daunting. Deep reds and royal blues mingled with pale creams and light grays. The gray was the most serviceable choice with less decoration along the hems, but the blue was too irresistible. She pulled the tunic gown over her head, instantly feeling like a princess. Or, rather, like a duchess. That is what the queen called her earlier, right? Lady Aeron, the High Duchess of Draig, wife to the Duke.

"More like wife to an arrogant, overbearing pain in my…" Her words became distracted as she stroked the sleeve of the gown. The material was so

HIS HIGHNESS THE DUKE

soft. She'd never worn anything quite like it. The skirts were slender compared to the other gown she'd been given. Perhaps it was the lack of under dress, or the elegant cut of the material. It didn't matter. She couldn't quit twisting her waist back and forth to watch the skirt swish and mold against her legs.

She again touched her hair, feeling the mess with no way of seeing it for herself. She tried to comb her fingers through it.

"Did you not hear me?" the queen asked from the doorway. "Oh, lovely, you found the gowns. I trust they fit?"

Aeron nodded. "Yes, thank you."

"That one is an interesting choice for travel," the queen said. "I would have thought the gray. Ah, well, they are now yours to do with as you please. I've brought Mirox to satchel the remainder of the gowns. I'll wait until you're ready and then I'll take you to meet the duke by the stables. He is in the communications tower and will join you as soon as he is finished."

"We're leaving?" Aeron swallowed. So soon? She had thought she'd get at least one day without having to traipse all over the countryside. "Where are we going now?"

"Bron didn't tell you?" The queen eyed Aeron's

MICHELLE M. PILLOW

hair. "Oh, my, let's take care of that for you, shall we?"

"Tell me what?"

"You must have been sleeping. You looked very tired when we spoke earlier." The queen picked up a comb on a shadowed dresser and came forward. She made a motion commanding Aeron to turn. "You leave for your home. I would welcome you to stay here longer of course, but now is not a good time. The new marriages must settle. You understand, don't you?"

Aeron nodded. Did the queen mean her marriage to Bron? Was it clear to the queen that Aeron was unsettled?

"We must have you back. Perhaps the coronation dinner? I am sure the princes and princesses would love to meet you. They are," the queen paused in her work, "indisposed of at the moment."

"I understand," Aeron said politely, though she really didn't have the faintest clue as to what was happening with the Draig princes and princesses. She doubted anyone was going to explain it to her. Apparently, Bron couldn't even explain their travel plans.

To be fair, though, she had left him in a rather abrupt state. The thought made her smile. He deserved it. And, if he started talking to her like a servant, she'd do it again. The slight unfulfilled ache in her lower regions protested the plan. Walking away had been difficult. Luckily, she'd had her anger to fuel her retreat.

She glanced longingly at the bed. Still, it would have been nice to have him coming to her bed, begging her to forgive…

The queen tugged the comb at her tangled hair, pulling it. Aeron bit her lip.

"There." The queen handed over the comb. "Better."

BRON LOOKED LONGINGLY at the practice field where his cousin, Prince Zoran, threw blades at some of the younger soldiers. He remembered the game well. Each throw would get closer and closer until the soldier jumped back. The man who held his position the longest without letting the blade embed into his foot would win. There were a few men with scars on their feet, but a medic was always nearby if there were accidents.

Instead of joining in the exercise, he turned away from the practice yard toward one of the palace's secret tunnels. Going several feet into the mountain, through the bare passageway, he greeted the young soldier guarding the elevator. With very

MICHELLE M. PILLOW

few words, the man let Bron pass the checkpoint. The young soldier pushed a button and they began to rise with lightening speed, as they took an elevator up to the communications tower. The tower was located at the top of the mountain in a manmade-like pyramid. From the bottom of the mountain and from space, the peak was camouflaged to look like the red rock. However, inside, it was as transparent as glass. Not even ship sensors from space would be able to detect its location— unless of course someone made an unauthorized communication during the wrong time of day. If atmospheric conditions were just right overhead, a communication wave meant for the outer galaxy could be traced to the palace source. It was an acceptable risk as precautions were taken against such things.

"Inform Jorne," Bron said to the young soldier.

"Yes, my lord," the man answered.

Bron stopped near a man who worked next to a floating screen. His fingers tapped the air, causing it to change and flicker with new information. "New equipment?"

The man glanced back and nodded. "Installed three months ago. Faster interface and portable." He pressed a small device on the desk. The screen disappeared into it. The man picked up the device and bounced it in his hand. "Durable. Handy for

HIS HIGHNESS THE DUKE

transporting information. The king has ordered we test it." The man set it back down and pressed the button twice. The screen reappeared.

Bron nodded in approval. "With the king's approval, I would like to see the system specs when you are done with your test."

"Yes, my lord," the man agreed. He turned back to work.

Bron looked up at the sky. Through the solar shielding on the panels, he could see an expanse of stars normally hidden by daylight.

"My lord," Jorne said, coming into the tower from his private office. The man was taller than Bron but of slenderer build. He had lived for nearly four hundred years, three hundred and eight of those in service to the royal family.

Bron gestured toward Jorne's office. The man nodded and led the way into the private area and closed the metal door behind them.

"The king sent me," Bron began. He quickly told the man the situation before adding, "You are to tell no one of this. If an unauthorized ship comes close to our airspace, you are to report directly to the king, and to me or one of my brothers. This information is uncertain."

"As you wish, my lord." Jorne nodded.

Bron spoke to the man awhile longer, asking after his family. His last son had found a bride at the ceremony and was, according to his proud father, well matched and incredibly happy. Apparently the new couple was already speaking of having children. Bron smiled politely and swallowed down the bitter taste of his jealousy.

He rode the elevator back down alone. The early morning air greeted him as he stepped back outside. Zoran barked orders in the distance.

Bron had spent the night on the circular couch, listening to the sound of his wife's breathing in the next room. Aeron slept deeply, barely moving. He had not been so lucky.

When the queen's servant delivered several gowns with the dawn, he'd placed them on the table in Aeron's room. She seemed so peaceful that he hadn't wanted to wake her. Now, knowing the queen would have her fed and delivered to the stables to meet him, he hesitated. He gave a wistful glance at the exercise field. Battle sounded easier than facing an angry wife.

From the ground, because of the angle, it was impossible to see the windows or balconies of the palace that adjoined the royal family and guest quarters. They were carved just so, that even from a distance it looked just like a mountain cliff. Within the surrounding valley, near where the breeding festival grounds had been, nestled a small village under the protection of the House of Draig.

HIS HIGHNESS THE DUKE

The roads were of rocky earth, smoothed flat and even. The village was kept immaculately clean, built with almost a military perfection of angles. The houses were of rock and wood, so that even the poorest of families were well provided for.

The royal stables overlooked the village. It was a rustic, rectangular structure filled with some of the finest ceffyl stock on the planet. The stableman waited next to his wife. For a moment, he stopped walking. She didn't see him as she spoke to the man. A whisper of a smile graced her features. She had always been beautiful to him, but seeing her dressed as a noblewoman in the fine dark blue gown given to her by the queen, he felt his breath catch. The color played off her features, adding a rich hue to her black hair and lighting her blue eyes with an inner fire, magnifying the color.

Seeing the stableman looking at him, he again began to walk. Aeron's eyes turned to him. Her smile held its place. Then, as if catching herself staring, she glanced to the ground and back up at the stableman.

"My lord," the stableman greeted. "I was just giving my lady a message for Lord Alek. I have taken the ceffyl out of isolation and she is doing much better. The solarflowers have worked their way out of her system and she is again eating normally."

MICHELLE M. PILLOW

Bron nodded. He didn't know the exact situation the stableman was referring to, but it wasn't unusual to get messages from his brothers. Was that the conversation that had put a smile on his wife's face? Ceffyl care? "I will tell him. Thank you."

The stableman's eyes drifted once more to the new duchess before he moved back to the stall. If Bron wasn't mistaken, the man actually started to whistle.

"Has something happened?" Aeron studied him carefully. Her smile was gone and back was her serious look of concern.

"Overnight?" Aeron laughed, but the sound was humorless. He thought of his long, unfulfilled night on the couch. "No. Nothing. Absolutely nothing."

"Ah." She relaxed. "I thought maybe, from your expression, that the Tyoe might have done something."

The Tyoe. Of course, that is what she was thinking about. That is all she ever seemed to be thinking about. Bron suddenly found himself very jealous of this mysterious, technologically advanced, conquering alien race. He willed one of them to attack just so he could punch the creature in the face and relieve some of his frustration. He glanced at the green-tinted sky. No such luck.

"They gave us Ugly again," Aeron said,

HIS HIGHNESS THE DUKE

pointing at her ceffyl. She actually reached out to touch the animal's back and patted it lightly. "The stableman asked if you were going to want the same mount, that big beast we took from Alek. I told him that was probably fine since that was the animal you rode in on, but I wasn't sure how the system works. Do you just take any animal from any stable that you want?"

"It is fine," Bron said, even though Alek's beast was a temperamental creature that needed a consistently firm hand from its rider. Not exactly the top choice in the stables. "Most of the ceffyls belong to my family, but the royal family uses them as they see fit in exchange for taking care of them. It is an old system, but it works well enough for all."

Automatically, he helped her onto her mount. When she was balanced and her dress arranged around her legs, he mounted his steed and directed it to move with a light tug of the center horn. The creature obeyed and began lumbering forward. Aeron's beast followed him. Out of the corner of his eyes, he saw her studying his hand as if trying to mimic his movements.

They rode along the far edge of the practice field, up the overlooking cliff toward the mountain paths. As the way widened, he moved his mount to the side to let her ride next to him.

"Do your people always travel this much?" Aeron asked.

"This much?"

"I have been on a ceffyl everyday since I've come to your planet. I just wondered if it was normal." She adjusted on her seat, stretching her back and arms while trying to maintain balance.

Bron hid his smile as he stared forward. "No. It is not usual."

"I am glad to hear it. I do not think my body can take much more of this bumping around." She adjusted uncomfortably on the animal's back, as if to prove her point.

There was nothing he could do to make the ride easier for her. "When we get home, we will be able to get some rest."

"Home," she repeated softly. He felt a wave of sadness wash over him from her. Their connection was growing and he wasn't sure how to stop it, or if he even wanted to. Her sadness tormented him, but without the connection he wouldn't have been able to detect the emotion within her.

"I desire you," he said, stopping himself. Clearing his throat, he said louder, "I desire that you should be happy with your new home. Whatever comfort you need, I will find a way to get it for you. Life on this world is not as rough as you may think. We do have technology, if that is what you need to be happy. What we don't have, I will find. All you have to do is ask."

She looked at him in surprise. "Did I complain? I did not mean to give the impression—"

"No, you have not complained, but I can sense the dissatisfaction in you," he said. The mount, sensing his tension, tried to go faster. Bron forced the creature to slow to a steady pace.

"Dissatisfaction?" she repeated, slowly. She stared at his face. "So what the queen said is true. We will be able to feel each other. I've had this really strange feeling washing over me since I saw you at the stables. It's..." Aeron closed her eyes. Bron felt her trying to pry back the mental blockades he had constructed to keep her out. With a sigh, he opened himself to her. She gasped. "I feel concern. Not fear, but... concern? Is that right?" She shook her head, confused. "Are you concerned about the Tyoe?"

He didn't want to answer. No, not the Tyoe. "I feel your sadness. I know you are not happy here. I am sorry for it. Just name it and whatever happiness I can give you will be yours. Food simulators. Servants. Dresses. Jewels. Swords. Lasers. Computers. Medic Units..."

"Respect," she inserted when he took a breath.

That surprised him, but he could tell she was serious. In the process of trying to feel inside of

MICHELLE M. PILLOW

him, she'd opened herself to his inner inspection. He stopped the ceffyl and turned back toward the palace. "Who disrespected you? I will deal with it at once."

"Bron," she said.

Anger rippled through him. He should have been by her side.

"Bron, stop!" She hadn't moved to follow him. The beast protested as he urged his mount back around to where she waited. "I meant you. Respect from you."

He felt as if she'd slapped him. No, he would have preferred that she slapped him. This was much worse.

"If I made you feel disrespected, I will atone for it immediately," he answered. What else could he say? "I will find a temple and—"

"Don't be dramatic," she broke in. "An apology will suffice."

"I apologize," he said instantly.

"You don't even realize what you did, do you?" She sighed. "The Tyoe situation. I am the one who brought you the information. Without me, you wouldn't even know about it, but then you dismiss me repeatedly when I ask about it. You tell me that you will handle things."

"I will handle—"

"You said I, not *we*." She pointed at him and

HIS HIGHNESS THE DUKE

then herself and then back at him. "We. I am part of this. I gave up everything I knew to come here because of this. I had a life. It might not have been exciting or adventurous, but it was mine and it was safe. You seem to be under the impression that when I came here, my life began. The truth is, my life started to end when I came here. The moment we came together in the tent, my biological clock began to tick. I'm dying, Bron. It is the curse of my people. When a female has sex, she begins to die. Otherwise, I would have lived forever. So when you dismiss me like I'm some simple woman who needs protected from the details of what's happening, I get insulted. In a roundabout way, I gave up my life for this possible battle. I gave it up to save your world. So if I annoy you by asking about the alien threat too much, or am persistent, that is why. I want my last acts to mean something. So, when you say you will handle it and dismiss me, I feel very disrespected."

She became very animated as she spoke. Bron instantly swung down from his mount and went toward her. "Dying? Are you …?" He searched her for signs of pain, but saw none. He sniffed the air. She didn't smell sick. In fact, she smelled sweet.

"Yes. I don't have much time. So you can see why I need you to tell me about the Tyoe."

"How much time do you have? There must be

221

someone I can call. The palace doctor. A medic? The Medical Alliance for Planetary Heath—they will have an answer."

"Maybe fifty years," she answered mournfully.

"Fifty…" He frowned.

"I know. I'm sorry." She didn't move off her ceffyl.

His frown deepened. He would have asked her if she was joking, but he could see she was serious. "Is that not the normal lifespan of a human?"

"Earth human, yes, but my people were not from Earth. We are immortal until we have sex."

He breathed deeply. "You smell very human to me."

"I am human, just a different kind of…" She frowned and moved to slide off the animal's back. "You think I'm lying about this? What possible reason would I have to make up such a thing?"

"No, I know you are not lying, but perhaps you are… mistaken?" He automatically lifted his hands to help her down. "If you are human, this concern is not valid. When you became my wife we became joined. Our—"

"The queen already told me about the whole sharing years thing, but I don't think it will work with me. We might have been young at the time, but my sister and I remember very clearly what our mother said. When a woman has sex, her biological clock begins to tick and she begins to die. The species must go on, and that is why motherhood must be carefully considered and—"

Bron sighed with relief, believing to understand. "You were young?"

Aeron frowned. "Yes.

"You are not dying." He reached to cup her face. "Your mother was trying to keep you from attracting the attention of boys."

"My mother was not a liar. My grandmother and aunts and cousins were not liars. We all knew the…" she paused and took a deep breath. "It was the last thing my mother…"

His expression fell. "Last? How old were you when you lost her?"

"I was sixteen years when we lost them all," she said bitterly.

"All? Was there an accident? Like a mine collapse?" He reached for her but she shied away from him.

"I guess it doesn't matter anymore." Aeron paced away from the ceffyls. The animals took the opportunity to start grazing along side of the road. They licked at plant blades, pulling them into their mouths. "My home was destroyed. Not just my actual home, but my whole planet. The Gregori had a weapon, a very big weapon, and they wanted to test it. My planet was conveniently located.

MICHELLE M. PILLOW

That's it. Convenient. Their ship didn't even land. It just bored a laser drill into the surface and ignited the core. It happened so fast. We, my sister Riona and I, were in space. We were on our way back home after an educational trip to the Zonar District. The only consolation was the resulting blast blew apart the Gregori ship and it was destroyed. Apparently it was in direct line with an energy factory. Bad luck for them. There was no way to calculate how the energy blast from that factory would have projected. The Federation looked into it, but it was determined everyone involved was already dead. That is why I originally applied to work at the Federation, to see their investigative reports. They called it a tragedy and that was it. Everything I knew was gone and it was simply a tragedy with no one living to blame."

"You're Jagranst?" Bron had remembered hearing tales of the planet that died. She stiffened, but nodded. "My brother, Mirek, heard variations of the story from different travelers when he was in space doing ore negotiations. I did not know there were survivors. We weren't even sure the stories were true. They sounded like a scary tale told to frighten. I'm sorry that happened to you, Acron. I did not know."

It was no wonder she was so desperate to help his people. He couldn't imagine seeing his home,

HIS HIGHNESS THE DUKE

his people, his planet, destroyed before his eyes with nothing to be done about it but watch and live on. Had he lived through that, only to discover that it might happen again, there was nothing he wouldn't do to stop it.

"Riona and I are all that is left," she said. "I didn't mean to get into this conversation. It has no real relevance to stopping the Tyoe or the fact I'm dying."

Bron felt her concern, her fear, her sadness. So much was made clearer with her story. He was a man of action and, as such, he would take the only action he could. Right now, that would be to comfort his wife by taking control of the situation. "We don't know that you are dying." Just saying it caused his gut to tighten, but the warrior in him refused to just accept that as her fate. "I will give every year I have to ensuring you are with me. If you are to die, we will die together. I gave you my years, Aeron. I will not take them back now."

Fifty years was a long time in some ways, but when compared to an eternity, he could see how she would feel she didn't have much time. It would have to be enough. If that is all they had, it would be enough. He could not imagine living without her. It was that simple.

Bron wanted nothing more than to pull her into his arms and keep her safe. Every instinct told him to protect her like the delicate creature she appeared to be. But there was a strength in her, born from tragedy and impossible to ignore. "It is too soon to give up hope. Whatever time the gods give us, we'll take. But one thing we Draig know how to do is fight. Whatever comes, whatever needs to be done, we'll do it. Together."

Aeron took a deep breath. Her heart raced. She didn't look at Bron, couldn't, not yet. A strange relief washed over her as she told him the truth. The past was hard to face, but telling him hadn't been as difficult as she imagined.

A hand pressed against her shoulder. "What you feel is relevant. It is why you came here. It is why you are trying to save my people from a threat we didn't know existed. You have given us the chance your people never had. Because of you, we are aware and we will be ready."

She gave a small laugh. A tear rolled over her cheek from her watery eyes and she wiped it away. Aeron turned to him. His face was so open, so calm and sure, yet there was concern in him too. She felt more than saw it. "I thought it was fate that brought me. The will of the gods."

"That, too," he assured her. The breeze tousled

his hair, pressing against his handsome face. She lifted her hand, brushing back a strand of dark brown hair to uncover his eyes. "None of us know how long we have to live. Do not spend your days feeling as if you are dying."

The words might have sounded like a command, but they were soft and pleading. There were things she wanted to say to him, but she didn't know where to start. She'd already told him so much. She hadn't planned it. The words had just rolled out of her like she couldn't keep it all inside anymore.

"If there is a way, I will save you from that fate." He cupped her cheeks, turning her face toward his. "By all the gods, I will find a way to keep you with me or we die together."

"There is no reason for you to die if I—"

Bron's kiss cut her words off. The warm pressure of his mouth drew her in. She was mesmerized by him, pulled by every fiber in her being to be closer to him, to explore the feelings reeling inside her, inside him. It became impossible to decipher which were hers and which were his. The sensations were overwhelming, but how could she fight such passion, such desire? She felt wanted, needed. It was in his words, in his touch.

Mindless as to where they were, she pulled on his clothes, wanting to be closer. His hands formed against her back, inching her skirt up by the fistful. Aeron lifted his tunic to expose his waist. The warmth of his flesh heated her cooler fingers. She turned her face to his neck, kissing and biting the skin beneath his ear. She breathed deeply, taking in his scent.

She kissed her way back up his jaw. He whispered in her ear, but she couldn't understand the Draig words. His hands seemed to be everywhere at once, on her waist, her back, touching the exposed backs of her thighs. She unfastened his pants, wishing there was a way to get him completely naked. In a moment of sanity, she realized they were on the side of a mountain path, outside, displayed for whoever happened by.

She tried to pull her mouth away to express her concerns, but his lips stayed insistently against hers. All thoughts fled as his tongue massaged her lips in a deft stroke. Aeron thrust her hand down the front of his pants, finding the stiff erection straining and ready. The fact that he wanted her as much as she wanted him excited her. He was inside her mind. She heard his impassioned words begging her for more, but his mouth was busy on hers. Her thoughts whispered back to him, "Yes."

Bron growled, as if he actually heard what she was thinking. He broke his mouth free and instantly knelt on the ground. Looking up at her, he pulled at

HIS HIGHNESS THE DUKE

her hand, urging her to come over him as he leaned back. Aeron straddled his waist. She glanced over the mountains and valley surrounding them. She couldn't see anyone watching, but that didn't mean they weren't there.

Bron reached for her face and turned her focus back to him. "It is fine. There is no one."

She took him at his word. His eyes flashed with gold fire. A shiver worked over her. He pulled at her skirts and she lifted up. Hands fumbled and pulled in their eagerness. Finally, they were able to join. It wasn't like before. This time it felt different, more open. Their connection grew until she became part of him. The tip of him brushed against her. She gasped and bit her lip, tensing just a little in anticipation.

Bron took her by her hips and guided her down. She closed her eyes as the sensations of his claim overwhelmed her senses. His desire mingled with hers, her passion poured into him. It was insanity. It was perfect. Perfect insanity.

Aeron pressed her hands against his chest as she let him guide her thrusts. The position reminded her of that first night in the bridal tent. She'd been unable to stop herself. There had been something about him from the very beginning. As much as he frustrated her, she still wanted him. At first she had thought she'd thrown everything away for fleeting pleasure. Now, she didn't feel as if it was thrown away. Instead, she felt as if fate maybe had brought them together.

Her heart beat hard, thumping in her ears, outdone only by the soft groans and harsh pants coming from beneath her. The slow grind of his hips was enhanced by the pull of his hands. The pleasure built slowly. Neither of them rushed the climax. She loved these moments, the mindless sensation that blocked out everything else.

Aeron watched his face. Passion filled his expression, from the lids that fell heavy over his brown eyes to the part of his lips. His body strained. She detected the flex of his muscles beneath this clothing. She pulled at his tunic, exposing his stomach to touch his flesh. His thrusts became faster, more insistent. There was no stopping the onslaught of pleasure as it erupted between them. She tensed, closing her eyes as her head fell back on her shoulders.

By small, shivering degrees sanity returned. His breathing slowed, even as she still struggled to find her breath. He moved beneath her, prompting her to open her eyes and look at him. Bron rolled to sitting. The movement caused her to pull off him as she sat back on his legs. Before she could speak, he took her face and kissed her. He appeared very pleased by what had transpired. No, it was more than appeared. He was pleased. She felt it as surely as she felt her heartbeat only now starting to slow down.

"It is time I took you home, my lady," he said against her lips. "We have much yet to discuss."

12

AERON GUESSED that it was evening, though the green-tinted light barely changed. The air did cool some and she was glad for the long sleeves of her dress—even if the skirt was now dirty from her time on the ground. Thinking of it, she smiled to herself and glanced to Bron. He looked at her and winked. Her smile deepened.

Bron nodded forward as they came over an incline. She turned her attention to see what he indicated. Her smile froze on her face. Surrounded by steep mountains, narrow passes, and rocky crags dotted with lush plant life, a castle home stood out against the elements like a timeless fortress. She heard Bron speak, but it was hard to hear what he said as her heartbeat resounded loudly in her ears. This was it. Her new home.

Home.

The word caused her to shiver. An innate fear unfurled inside her. She looked up at the sky for a sign of any anomaly. Part of her expected a blast of fire to rain down on them. The sound of Bron's voice drew her attention back to the stone fortress before her. It didn't matter how strong the castle was. One blast from space could destroy everything. Or, more likely, in the case of the Tyoe, a full scale attack on the planet.

The castle was nestled in the valley, a mere front for the homes hidden within the mountain's base, according to Bron. The earth was red with streaks of gray through the stone. Bron steered his ceffyl toward the large rectangular structure of the stables. The animal opened its mouth, hissing as its long tongue slithered from between its lips.

"Many blessings, my lord," an older man said as they neared.

"Thank you, Cenek," Bron answered. "May I introduce to you my wife, Lady Aeron. My lady, this is one of our top ceffyl trainers, Cenek."

"My lady." The man nodded. He had a gruff face, but with the ghost of a smile that seemed to radiate from him even when it did not physically show. Aeron didn't answer. She couldn't. Her throat was tight with trepidation.

HIS HIGHNESS THE DUKE

"Have my brothers arrived?" Bron asked, as he moved to help Aeron off her mount.

"Lord Mirek is here with his bride," Cenek pulled both ceffyls' horns at once, sending them toward the stables as he stayed behind. "It is unfortunate."

"Mirek brought home a bride?" Bron seemed surprised by the news.

"Yes." Cenek nodded. "She is alive. Physicians have been to see her and more have been sent for. She is in isolation."

"Isolation?" Aeron asked, concerned. The thought drew her from her worried thoughts. "Is she contagious?"

"Alien disease, I think, my lady," Cenek answered. "The rest is for Lord Mirek to tell."

Cenek followed the ceffyls into the stables.

"Biological attack?" Aeron asked when they were alone. It would be a way to wipe out a planet's population while barely lifting a finger. At her words, Cenek paused briefly near the stables, but did not turn around.

"We will speak with Mirek." Bron offered Aeron his arm as he led her toward the front entrance to the castle. Unlike the palace, there were no guards waiting to greet them at the entryway. "If there was a reason to be concerned, he would

MICHELLE M. PILLOW

have sent word. I am sure the isolation is merely a precaution."

"It's quiet here." Aeron observed, looking around. At the palace there had been soldiers practicing in the field. The sound of their fighting could be heard mingling with the distant laughter and talk of the villagers in the valley. "Do others live in the castle?"

"Just the family. Servants sometimes sleep here if it is late and they do not wish to go home. There is a community near the mines and more families spread throughout the forest," Bron said. "As you can see from Cenek, we are not as formal as the palace. We prefer things to be simpler. Everyone knows their work and does it. They come and go as they please. In several months' time, we'll have a mining festival. This entire yard will be alive with celebration."

Though a series of iron gates had been built to block the entryway from attack, they were now retracted into the stone walls. No one stopped them from entering as they made their way inside. At first the entryway was dim, but as Bron led her forward a soft light began to glow from long strips in the wall.

"Daylight?" she asked, though it appeared to be the wrong color.

"Yes, filtered," he answered.

HIS HIGHNESS THE DUKE

Suddenly, the hallway split into five directions. Bron paused and pointed straight ahead. "The center hall will lead you to all the common rooms. Starting on the right, it is in order of birth. I am the oldest, so our hall is first. Then Alek, Mirek, and Vladan. Once you are inside, there are more hallways to learn and," he pointed over his head, "some above and below us as well. Try to stay on the main level until you know your way around. But, if you get lost, just close your eyes and think of me. I will find you or guide you back." He glanced upward. "Actually, now that we are married, we will be expected to move into the tower rooms. They were my parents' and we haven't used them since they passed."

"It's a maze?" Aeron stopped and eyed each path. They looked identical.

"It was designed this way to confuse intruders. If you go down a path and are not able to open a door once we scan you into the main system, you are heading down a dead end and should turn around. The outer halls spiral outward in an endless pattern to trap intruders. Should the interior sensors go down, any attackers would be dispersed into the sides of the mountain until they can be found and dealt with."

Aeron was about to ask more, but footsteps stopped her. She turned toward the entrance.

MICHELLE M. PILLOW

Instantly, she stepped closer to Bron and took his arm. Several very large men loomed before them, carrying long planks of industrial grade plastic and unmarked crates.

"My lord," a few of them said, seeing Bron, but they did not stop in their task. It took her a moment to remember which hall was which, but she realized they moved toward Mirek's home.

"That is industrial grade sheeting," Aeron said. "Do you think it's safe here? Your brother's bride must be really sick. No one was ill on the Galaxy Brides' ship. They would not have brought her on world if she had been."

"I did not think Mirek found a bride from the ship. Perhaps it is someone from his ambassadorial missions?" Bron asked more than answered. "There was a visiting bride not on the Galaxy Brides' ship, Lady Clara of Redding." Bron urged her to follow the workers. "Come. We will find out."

Bron held her hand to his arm. The hall twisted and turned, but they stayed on a steady course. Coming to a door with intricate patterns carved into the frame, Bron led her inside. The workers were already setting up their supplies at the far end of the home.

Mirek's living quarters were lavish, all smoothed stone walls and floors with thick rugs and

HIS HIGHNESS THE DUKE

wooden furniture. Like the palace, it was a home within the larger castle home. The oversized décor fit nicely into the spacious abode. A banner of a dragon standard hung on the wall. It's predominant placement gave away its importance.

Seeing a man who looked very much like Bron and Alek, she knew Mirek was home. Bron went to his brother. Mirek had the same medium brown hair that seemed to run in the family, but his eyes were a bright green. He looked tired, but it did not show in his movements as he gestured toward the room being renovated in his home. Office furniture was being moved out and the plastic sheeting moved in.

Couches were set in a square around a low table wrapped around a fire pit. A worker bumped past her and mumbled an apology. Since Bron was in deep conversation with his brother, she made her way to the couches to get out of the workers' way. Absently brushing at her skirt, she tried to get rid of the dirt stain. It really was a shame the blue was ruined. If she was lucky, they would have some kind of laser cleaner that could fix the material.

The workers had set some supplies on a couple of the couches. Aeron made her way past a large plastic crate. Glancing inside it as she passed, she froze in horror.

"Riona," she whispered. Aeron took a hesitant

MICHELLE M. PILLOW

step back. Her sister was locked inside the box. Riona's eyes were closed and it looked like she slept in forced stasis. Red patches of blisters created strange patterns on her flesh. Around those bumps the flesh was pale, too pale for Riona. The auburn length of her hair had been pulled and twisted on the top of her head into a very neat, very un-Riona-like bun. Aeron touched the cool transparent barrier blocking her sister from her. She tapped the industrial plastic, and whispered, "Riona?" Her sister didn't move. Aeron hit it harder with the flat of her palm. "Riona, wake up."

Almost as soon as she'd slapped the human crate, two men were on top of her pulling her back.

"Don't," Bron said.

"What do you think you are doing to my wife?" Mirek demanded. He stood near Riona's head, his arms spread as if to protect the sleeping woman.

"Me? What are you doing with my sister? She's supposed to be out gallivanting the star systems." Aeron turned, frowning with worry. "How did…? What did you do to her?"

"She is ill," Bron tried to explain.

"No. She was fine on the ship. She was healthy. We all had the scans. We…" Aeron swatted at Bron's hands, making him let her go. "We need to get her to a medical booth."

HIS HIGHNESS THE DUKE

"Riona is your sister?" Mirek asked, not as angry as before. He seemed doubtful.

"What did you do to her?" Aeron pushed past Mirek and leaned over her sister, seeing if she breathed. A tube stuck out of her side, filled with yellow liquid. A fine powder coated her skin. It was what made her look so pale. "Take her out of stasis. Wake her up. I want to talk to her."

"I can't. She won't wake up," Mirek answered. "The stasis is to keep her comfortable."

Somewhere in the back of her mind, Aeron knew she was being mean, but she couldn't help it. This was her sister. Riona was only on this planet because of her. "You can't be her husband. Husbands are supposed to protect wives on this planet. This can't be happening. Ri would never get married, would you?" Aeron stroked the box, wishing she could make it go away. None of this was right. A tear slid down her cheek to splash on the barrier. This time her words were for her sister, as she whispered, "What did you do? Ri, this is all wrong. You don't belong here."

"We are not sure what happened, but the physicians believe she had an allergic reaction to some plant life in the forest. She is stable, but for now it is best if she breathes filtered air. That is why we had her transferred to a stasis pod. I called in several favors to have one delivered here." Mirek looked at his brother. He sounded insistent, and a little defensive. "The builders are constructing a room for her. She will be moved just as soon as it is allowed. I have sent for more doctors and a new medic unit, but the medical booths are not working. I—"

"I know you are doing everything you can," Bron interrupted. He touched Aeron's arm. "Everything will be done for her. I swear it to you, Aeron."

"I will not leave her," Mirek said. "She will have every care taken."

Aeron gave him a dubious look. She didn't know him. The only thing he had in his favor was that he was related to Bron. She did, however, know her sister. There was no way Riona would be tricked into staying on this planet. Her sister was too smart for that.

"We will move her to my room. She can stay with me," Aeron said. "I will look after her."

"She must be with her husband," Bron disagreed.

"She needs a sterile room. This one is already being built," Mirek said. "I will take care of my wife."

Aeron glanced at him, thinking that he hadn't done a good job of it so far. Bron touched her again and she felt his surety, his calm. She slowly nodded. "Fine. But I will be here often to check on

HIS HIGHNESS THE DUKE

her. I want to read the medical reports so far. And I want to know exactly what happened. And I want to be here whenever she is examined. And I want life sign monitors in my room. And if you so much as touch her without her consent, I'll—"

Bron physically grabbed his wife and pulled her to his chest. He pressed her face hard into his tunic, cutting off her demands. Stroking her hair, he said very loudly, "Lady Aeron is worried about Lady Riona. They are sisters."

The sound of the workers murmuring in understanding caused Aeron to realize they were being listened to.

"Everything you ask will be done," Mirek said. If they had been talking about anyone else, Aeron might have felt sorry for the man.

Aeron opened her mouth, but Bron still had her pressed close. He broke in before she could speak, "You have both of our words. Your sister will have every comfort met."

When Bron said it, she felt assured. Slowly, she nodded in agreement. "Fine."

"Come," Bron insisted. "There is nothing to be done while the men work. Mirek, we will come back first thing in the morning to visit."

"You may visit her anytime," Mirek said. "I have nothing to hide. I will program your voice into my home. You may come and go as you please."

MICHELLE M. PILLOW

Aeron gave one last look at her sister as Bron urged her from the room. When they were alone in the hall, far away from the door to Mirek's home, he said, "My brother is a good man. He would not have harmed her. If he said she had a reaction to plant life, that is what happened."

"I did not say I doubted him," Aeron stated weakly, though in truth she was not sure all she had said aloud.

"Your expression spoke for you," he said. "You blame him."

"I was shocked to see her. Riona would not have taken a husband." Aeron shook her head in denial. "At all. If you thought I was stubborn about marriage, that is only because you haven't met Ri. She would never agree to settle down, even if she was in love. In fact, if she was in love, she'd probably sabotage the marriage because of it."

"Sabotage? Why would someone fight love?" Bron looked at his wife and pressed his lips tightly together, as if remembering their problems.

"When you see what we've seen, it changes you. So much loss in one moment. Everything changed. We lost our family, our people, our home, our belongings, our planet. I hid and Ri went out and lived life to the fullest, refusing to settle. There has been a fire under my sister's feet since the day she was born. Then, after the attack on our home world, that fire ignited under her whole body. She's been moving through the universe like a comet ever since. If she is here, it is not willingly. I would bet my life on it."

"My brother is honorable," Bron protested.

"And I know my sister." She felt his frustration, but she thought of her sister in a stasis chamber waiting on an isolation room. "I want those medical reports, Bron."

He frowned, but nodded. "It is late, my lady, and we have had a long journey. I will show you to your new home so you may eat and find rest. You will have your sister's medical reports by the morning."

To her surprise, she couldn't feel what he was feeling, at least not as strongly as before. She followed behind him as he walked through the corridors at a fast pace. He did not go the way they came, instead opening a side door with a hand scanner before taking halls and stairs and more doorways in a seemingly haphazard pattern. If she didn't keep up, there was no way she would find her way back out again.

AERON's new home was like nothing she'd ever seen before. She had been expecting it to be like

Mirek's but instead found a vastly different layout and design. Woven squares were fitted against the walls to hide the stone beneath. The main room was a giant oval with a hanging light fixture in the center. It reflected light from above, spreading it around the room. Semi-circle couches were next to the walls. The seats faced outward and were arranged around a center table.

In the middle of the room, two oversized couches formed a complete circle under the light fixture. The table in the very middle had seams running over the surface in what appeared to be a carved pattern. It might have looked like a decorative wooden table, but it was computerized. She knew her communications devices and the pattern had deep grooves where the transparent computer screens and holographic images would project from.

Before he left her alone, Bron revealed a food simulator hidden in the wall. It was an older model, but functioning. At her questioning look, he said, "On the occasion we entertain alien races in trade negotiations, it is helpful to be able to provide them with whatever they want."

Aeron didn't care what the reason was, she was just happy to not have to cook at the moment. She might not mind preparing food, but there was something to be said about the instant gratification

HIS HIGHNESS THE DUKE

of punching in an order and getting it automatically. Sure, it didn't taste the same, but after a lifetime of eating simulator food it was hardly unpalatable. Even as she thought it, she knew it wasn't necessarily true. The simulator couldn't compare to the flavor of freshly cooked meals.

Four doors were placed around the room. One went to the bathroom with a large carved tub much like the one in the palace. The second went outside to the halls. The others were to the kitchen and to an exercise room. Though the ceilings were two stories high in the main room, a balcony blocked off an open hall on the second floor. On the second story, doors led to more rooms.

Aeron materialized a bowl of bartal stew and waited for Bron to return. When he didn't appear, she took a bath, part of her hoping he would walk in on her. She regretted walking out on him at the palace. It would have been nice to explore him in the water—so warm and wet, gliding flesh. She gave a soft moan. It would have been heavenly.

When her fingers began to wrinkle from overexposure to the water, she wrapped her body in a drying linen and made her way upstairs. The rooms were all sleeping chambers, but only one looked to be ready for use. The oversized bed was a perfect square. She crawled in wearing the linen and snuggled beneath the covers. She didn't imagine she'd be able to sleep, but the inviting warmth was too much and her eyes drifted closed.

"I UNDERSTAND what you are asking me, but I can't leave my wife," Mirek said. "If it becomes necessary to leave, Vladan can go in my place. His marriage should be settled. We all saw the crystal glow when his wife chose him before the ceremony."

"He is married to an alien woman who does not appear as we do and who refused to follow our ceremonies. I would hardly call Vladan's marriage settled," Bron said. "We need you, Mirek. You know the travelers who visit our system. You have dealt with them. We need you to make subtle inquiries. Vladan is not always the most diplomatic. He is used to dealing with the miners."

Mirek sat by the head of his wife. He rested his hand on the top of her plastic prison. "You cannot ask me to go. Not now. I can't leave her like this."

"My wife will tend to her sister," Bron said. "We need to assess threat."

"I know the Tyoe," Mirek said. "They are an aggressive race."

"And you have never mentioned them?" Bron took the seat across from his brother. He had told

HIS HIGHNESS THE DUKE

him everything—his capture and imprisonment underground, Aeron's warning about the aliens, the king's orders.

"There was nothing to mention," Mirek said. "Normally, we do not deal with them. They offered to buy our mines for a very unfair price, and I refused. They are not the first to attempt such deals and they will not be the last. I daresay their offer was better than those who wish for us to continue to do the labor while they reap the profits. I don't know what intelligence you wish me to find out. I doubt there is anything worth finding. My dealings with them are logged in the records."

Bron watched Mirek's hand trace the outline of his sleeping wife's face, as if he could feel her through the transparent barrier. He couldn't imagine not being able to touch his wife. "It is unfair to ask it of you, brother."

"And I am honor bound to go if duty calls for it," he said softly. Mirek stared at his wife's unmoving face. If Bron didn't know better, he would have thought the woman dead. "I should not have tried to give Vladan my duties. I will make the necessary arrangements. Let me reach out to a few of my contacts. We were not planning a launch, so it will take a few days to get the ship ready and the pilot back here. We will scan the countryside from space and will also ensure no one is in orbit. A visual search will be much more efficient than the scans from on surface."

Bron nodded. He did not need to assure his brother that all that could be done would be done for Riona. Even if she wasn't Aeron's sister, the woman was family. When she married Mirek, she became one of them. They would each give their life to protect a family member. Or their fortunes to save her. Just as they would give everything to save Aeron. Bron studied Riona. If they were sisters, she would have the same issue. He thought about telling Mirek, but didn't want to give his brother more to be concerned about.

"Many blessings on your marriage, brother," Bron said. "I trust that fate will see your bride awaken from this sleep. If we have to send across the galaxy for a doctor, we will."

Mirek nodded. "I already have. You will have a copy of the medical files in the morning for your wife."

"Aeron does not understand our ways. She meant no insult—"

Mirek lifted his hand to stop Bron's words. "She fears for her sister. There is no explanation necessary."

Bron left his brother alone with the sleeping bride. The sight of them together haunted him. The gods would not give Mirek a woman just to take her away. They had to have faith that Riona would awaken in time.

Could it be the blessing of the ceremony was tainted somehow? The queen and king indicated that the princes were troubled in their choices. Vladan's bride was a strange creature with an odd-shaped head. Mirek's bride was ill and in isolation. If Riona was sick from the local flora and fauna, could she stay on world? Alek's marriage seemed to be in trouble. Alek and Kendall had been fighting last he saw them. And, his own marriage, though better, still felt shaky. He'd felt Aeron's earlier doubt when she'd looked at her sister. She did not trust them to do what they must.

He took the long route back to his home, going toward the entrance of the castle before turning to go back down the hall to his home. The slow walk gave him time to think, but it did little to settle his mind. He started listening for Aeron before he reached the entryway. All was quiet inside. As he went in, he focused his senses until he detected the sound of her steady breathing in their bedcham-bers. The sound was faint, but he knew she slept. Not wanting to wake her up and risk feeling the doubt and worry still undoubtedly radiating from within her, he went to the simulator to materialize food. He never used the thing for personal meals, but found he did not have the energy to prepare a meal for himself. The bland vegetables and flavorless meat tasted more like a punishment than a meal. Next came a bath and then several electronic files that needed his attention.

As the hours crept toward dawn, he knew he could avoid it no longer. Bron made his way upstairs to the dark bedroom. He did not let his eyes shift as he moved through the darkness. If he saw Aeron, he would have to touch her and her breathing was so peaceful and steady. Already her smell surrounded him, so sweet and feminine.

Bron crawled into bed and closed his eyes. Every nerve seemed to reach for her, but he kept his arms back. For now, he would be content to simply lie in her presence and listen to the sound of her sleep.

13

Five days passed in a blur of castle tours by one of the servants, visits to see Riona, contemplative looks from Bron, stoic looks from Mirek, and a flurry of workers and tailors. If she had been a suspicious woman, she would have thought Bron was avoiding her. In truth, there was no way to be sure. Yes, she needed dresses so the tailors were necessary. She did need to know how to get around the castle, and wanted to visit her sister even if Riona couldn't answer back.

Workers built Riona's isolation chamber, laboring endlessly until it was completed. Her sister was still in stasis. The medical reports were quite thorough, some even repetitive. That fact surprised Aeron. Mirek had every available physician in the Draig territory look at her sister. It would seem he really did care about her. Married to a Draig of her own, she was slowly coming to understand how these men worked. Whatever the reason, breaking the crystal really did seem to cement their feelings toward their wives. And, just perhaps, it also solidified the wives' feelings for their husbands—it just took a little longer.

Aeron watched Bron through the thick plastic door as he waited inside the isolation room with his brother. The workers left, filtering out of the home. She could hear them talking just beyond her sight, waiting in case they were needed. Mirek pushed a command on the wall panel to start the decontamination of the room.

The small room was built as some sort of laboratory. Hand-held medics, injector refills and other, more primitive, medicines lined the transparent cabinet on the wall. The only furniture was the medical bed next to the stasis pod. When the room finished cycling, they moved to open the pod. Aeron bit her lip, watching as they lifted her sister out of the plastic box and onto the medical bed.

The room didn't look like anything else she'd seen on the planet. It was too technically advanced. The fact that such drastic measures were needed just to maintain her sister's current state terrified Aeron. They lived in an age where medical booths

HIS HIGHNESS THE DUKE

could cure just about anything. If a booth couldn't help Riona, then…

Aeron didn't want to think about it. She couldn't lose her sister. Bron helped adjust Riona's limbs before moving toward the door. It opened and he quickly stepped out, leaving Mirek and Riona behind. The sickeningly sweet smell of decontamination followed him.

"What's he doing?" Aeron asked, pushing to see a clearer picture of Mirek before the door closed.

"The blisters cover her body. He needs to remove her clothing so they do not hamper her healing and reconnect her nutrient tube to the medical bed. Once she's stabilized, the tube can be removed. The doctors believe this is her best chance at recovery. The medical bed will monitor her for pain, and apply the necessary medications. The second she wakes up, Mirek's alarm will go off and he will inform us. Until that time, there is nothing more we can do."

Aeron placed her hand on his chest. It was one of the first moments of contact they'd had in the last several days. He had been keeping his distance, coming to the rooms late and leaving early. She assumed he had duties to attend to, but found she didn't like his schedule—even if he did send a servant to take her around the castle and entertain her.

MICHELLE M. PILLOW

"Thank you for all you have done," she said softly.

"Come, let's leave him to tend his wife." Bron took Aeron by the arm. "You look tired. Have you been sleeping?"

Before she could answer, they reached the workers. Bron said something to them in the Draig language. They immediately dispersed toward the front entryway.

"I really need to learn the language," she muttered.

"I will teach you, though I am told with your delicate vocal chords, it can be difficult for non-shifters to form the sounds." He lightly touched her throat and she shivered.

"Perhaps, but it would be nice to understand the sounds even if I can't form them. And to answer your question, no, I haven't been sleeping well. I keep trying to wait up for you. Is your schedule always so busy? Or are you avoiding me?" She meant it as a joke, but as she said the words, she couldn't help but feel the true fear in them.

"I only wanted to give you space. You appeared upset about your sister and..." He stopped himself. She wondered what he was going to say.

Closing her eyes, she felt the answer instead. "You felt my worry and mistook it for questioning your family's honor."

256

HIS HIGHNESS THE DUKE

He hesitated before finally nodding in agreement.

"And that insulted you."

Again, he hesitated and then nodded.

"Bron, I wish you would understand that I don't mean my worry to be insulting. It is not that I don't trust you to do the right thing, it's just that I am worried. I worry about everything—the Tyoe, my sister, you, us. It's just my way. I worry about things that I care about. I even sometimes worry about things I shouldn't care about. A Federation doctor once told me it was because of what happened. I couldn't control that one thing so now I worry when I can't control even the littlest of things. I'm also slow to accept change. The Federation didn't care because it made me good at my job. I looked at all the little details. It's just my way. I'm not sure I can change it."

"And you care about me?" A small smile lifted on the side of his face.

"How can you even ask me that?" She hit his arm lightly.

"So you are saying, all this worry I feel in you every time I come near you this last week is because you care? Not because you doubt me and my family's honor?"

"She's my sister, Bron. Of course I'm worried about her. She's the last of my people. I love her.

To see her like that, to be helpless to do anything, of course I worry for her." When he would speak, she stopped walking and added, "I know you will do all that you can for her and I appreciate that. I see the honor in you and in your brother. I don't doubt that. This ability to feel inside each other is new, for both of us. I think it will take time to decipher what it is we are sensing."

"It will come in time," he assured her. "As will other things."

"You mean dealing with the Tyoe?"

"There is no immediate threat, but we will be ready for it. One of our pilots will arrive tomorrow. Mirek will join the launch and check out things from space. He will scan the planet and ensure we are safe. Then he will send out transmission inquiries to friends. We will learn everything there is to discover about the Tyoe. If there is to be a battle in our future, we will be ready. Our people owe much to their new duchess. Perhaps someday they will know fully what it is you have done for them."

"Just keep them safe," she answered. "I don't care if they know. As far as I'm concerned, so long as we keep them safe it is enough."

Bron smiled at her. "Spoken like a true Draig."

"I can tell you one thing." Aeron's face turned red as she looked down.

"What is it?"

"I am pretty sure what you are feeling now is desire." She glanced up at him.

"Are you sure? I thought that was what you were feeling." He grinned, the look endearingly wicked and completely self-confident.

"I'm pretty sure that is you," she countered, running her hands up his chest.

"Hmm." He reached down, sweeping his arm under her legs. "Perhaps we should go home and sort out these feelings. I promise to get to the bottom of them if it takes all night."

"But…" She glanced around the hall. "Isn't it morning? I thought I finally had a handle on the time."

"Oh, it is morning. I just plan on this chore taking all night."

Aeron laughed as he walked faster, carrying her toward their home.

Bron traced a line down his wife's arm, watching as tiny little bumps formed in his finger's wake. He found himself mesmerized by the reaction. In fact, he was mesmerized by everything about her. He wondered if she knew how much control she had over him. One word, one thought, and he would be hers to command.

Aeron opened her eyes and gave him a sleepy smile before closing them once more and snuggling into his naked chest. The room was dark and he wondered if she could see his face. He doubted it.

Bron snaked his hand over her waist and held her close. Her soft skin molded easily to the will of his fingers. A ghost of a smile formed on her mouth at his touch.

"Ask," she murmured, suppressing a tiny yawn.

"Ask?" He ran his hand down to cup her ass before pulling at the back of her thigh. Her leg slid over his. He pressed his erection forward.

Aeron chuckled. "Not that. Ask me whatever it is you've been thinking about."

"But…" He rocked his hips forward.

"Fine, the answer to that question is yes, *after* you ask me the other question." She didn't shy away from his touch.

"You are an expert at communications." He rubbed his hand over her butt and back of her thigh. By all the stars, she was supple.

"That is a statement." She poked his chest.

"Leading to a question." He grinned, able to smell himself on her skin. It was highly erotic, like she was marked as his. "We need to set up communications between our home, the cabin, the mines,

HIS HIGHNESS THE DUKE

the village, and the palace. The units we have in place are old and some need repairs. I had hoped that with your knowledge you might like to oversee the project. I understand if you would rather not because it is a big undertaking. However, you do not seem the type to stay at home cooking and having babies—though I would be lying if I didn't say I had hopes of some of that, too. Would this be something you could help me on?"

Aeron slowly let go of her captured breath and nodded. "Yes. I would love to." She began to sit up from the bed, using his chest for leverage. "I'll need to see some maps and calculate distance. I'll also need to see the schematics for the current systems, know my budget, and—"

"Not at this moment, my lady," Bron said, pulling her back into his arms. "I believe you promised me something first."

Aeron laughed. "Yes."

"Yes." He nodded before kissing her throat. "Yes."

"Mmm," she sighed softly. Her hands found their way into his hair as she pulled him closer. His lips trailed over her shoulder, wherever they could reach. "Yes."

He made love to her slowly, tenderly, taking time to explore every inch of her. Already he had her body memorized, but each touch felt like the first. By the time he rolled on top of her, her legs were open and her sex wet and inviting. He kissed her as he entered her. Her hands roamed his body, tracing his muscles and scratching lightly at his flesh. Oh, but it was sweet, being inside his wife. Bron was sure he'd never felt anything so perfect.

In these moments, the world faded away and nothing else mattered. He was wrapped in her feelings for him, so open and pure. She didn't try to hide and neither did he. She could have all of him and he wouldn't stop her.

When they climaxed, it was in perfect, unspoken unison. He withdrew his lips from hers, letting her inhale deep breaths. Her heart beat so loud he could hear it. Her hands dropped along his arms as she rested her elbows on the bed.

Bron grinned. Pleasure erupted throughout him. "I love you, too, wife."

"But," she began in protest. "Too? You really should wait for me to say things out loud before you read my thoughts for me." Then, closing her eyes and breathing deeply, she returned his smile. "I love you, too, husband."

14

EPILOGUE

BRON SMILED to himself as he reached his feelings out to his wife. Their connection had grown stronger over the last several weeks. He could detect her almost anywhere in the castle. Sensing a wave of sadness and worry inside Aeron, he knew she was with her sister. Riona was still in stasis. There had been no change to her condition. All the doctors could tell them was to wait. They hoped she would simply wake up one day on her own. Until then, Mirek guarded and watched over her like a sacred treasure.

Sighing, he closed his eyes and rested his head on the back of his chair. Mirek's expedition into space had been most telling. There were signatures of another spacecraft in their area, both in the sky

MICHELLE M. PILLOW

and in the mountains, but no ship to connect it to. Whoever had kidnapped him had left their airspace. It would seem his wife was right. The Tyoe planned something. Perhaps his capture had been an experiment to see how they would react. Or perhaps the Tyoe had simply wanted to get rid of the highest ranking nobleman dealing with the mines. If that was the case, none of his family was safe. Precautions were already being taken.

At least his marriage was settled. In that he was grateful. Aeron still worried over her lifespan and his, though she did try to hide that fear from him. Bron was not convinced there was something to be worried about, but he had the doctors looking into it nonetheless. He would do whatever it took to protect his wife and put her at ease. In the meantime, she kept herself busy setting up the communication networks. Her knowledge far surpassed his in that area, and he was glad not to have to deal with encoding problems and distance modules.

As for Alek, Vladan and the four princes, those were entirely different stories that would take too long to decipher and tell. Bron did not have that kind of time or energy. Not today. Not when his wife had softly whispered to him in the early morning hours that she was pregnant.

Bron grinned. He was to be a father. Now, if

only his brothers and cousins could follow his example and get their marriages into order, life would be perfect.

The End

THE SERIES CONTINUES...

**Need more Dragon Lords?
The books continue!**
Dragon Lords 6: The Stubborn Lord

Want to see how King Attor's sons turn out, despite their father's teachings?
Lords of the Var®: The Savage King

Want to see how the King and Queen met?
Dragon Lords 9: The Dragon's Queen

THE SERIES CONTINUES...

Read all the Dragon Lords and Var books? Yay, you, keep going!

Space Lords 1: His Frost Maiden

Dragon Lords and *Lords of the Var®* in Modern Day Earth?

Captured by a Dragon-Shifter: Determined Prince

THE STUBBORN LORD

BY MICHELLE M. PILLOW

The Series Continues...

Dragon Lords Book 6

Bestselling Shape-shifter Romance

Repossessed...

Kendall Haven's life turns upside down when she's kidnapped off her fueling dock home by thugs claiming to have the right. Her father, the gambler, used her to cover his losses at the Larceny Casino Ship. Drugged and treated like cargo, she's sold to the highest bidder—Galaxy Brides Corporation.

Landing on a primitive planet on the far edge of the universe, she has no intention of fulfilling her father's contract—even if that contract includes marriage to a very handsome, very sexy, very intense barbarian of a man. He might be everything a woman fantasizes about, but he wants a little more than she can give.

Possession...

Lord Alek, Younger Duke of Draig, has not been lucky in finding his life mate. Resigned to a lonely life, he attends the bridal ceremony out of familial duty. Then the impossible happens—Kendall. Nothing goes according to tradition, but he can't let that dissuade him. She is his only chance at happiness, and no matter how she protests, he's not going to let her get away.

The Stubborn Lord Excerpt

He reached for his neck, jerking the crystal that hung there. The leather strap broke. Fingering the stone, he traced over the familiar surface before balling it into his fist. He thought about leaving it on the forest floor, as if his failure would be easier to bear without the constant reminder hanging about his neck. As he debated the decision his fist became warm, then hot. Loosening his grip, he saw

THE STUBBORN LORD

the faint glow of light radiating from between his fingers.

The crystal glowed.

Alek couldn't believe what he was seeing so he merely stared at it. He was in the forest. Alone.

Alone?

He held his breath and let the hard, dark brown flesh of the dragon work its way from his thighs up his body. A ridge grew from his forehead to create a protective shield over his nose and brow. Fangs extended in his mouth and talons grew from his nail beds. In his dragon form, he moved with greater agility and his senses were enhanced.

Was he alone? Was this the final word of the gods?

The crystal's light grew. The sign was unmistakable. His bride had to be near. Even as he thought it, he began to feel her inside him. The pull of her drew him before he picked up the sound of her breathing in the forest. Footfalls hit in a steady rhythm for several paces only to grow softer and slower. The beast inside him surged into action. He tracked her as easily as prey.

He found her standing alone in the dark, body pressed tight against a fallen log. Her widened brown eyes darted around the forest in fear. He stopped across the clearing from her. She didn't see him even though she looked in his direction several times. Alek took advantage of the moment to study her. Blonde hair fell about her shoulders. The ends were tipped with a dark red. She seemed so fragile and scared. A wave of protectiveness surged within him.

"Hayo? I can hear you breathing," she whispered. "Please show yourself. I can hear you."

Alek lifted his hand and opened his fist. The soft glow of the crystal alighted on his face. The woman found him instantly. He expected her to feel the same rush of pleasure he did. Instead, she started to scream.

The woman tripped on vines as she tried to get away from him. Her back slid along the tree trunk. He smelled the moss she disturbed in her haste. She kept her eyes on his and her arms outstretched as if that would keep him from attacking. Her feet worked frantically against the ground, pushing her back up the tree while trying to untangle her shoes from the forest floor.

"Please, no, no, no," she whimpered. "I don't belong here. Who are you people? You're supposed to be humanoids. The uploads said you were shaped like humans."

Alek tried to answer her, but the sound of his native tongue only seemed to terrify her more. He realized he was still shifted. No wonder she frightened. He'd been so eager to find her that he

THE STUBBORN LORD

hadn't bothered to change back. His people did not make their shifting abilities too widely known, and they hadn't revealed them to the researcher who'd originally interviewed his people for the uploads she spoke of.

"I don't understand." She pressed harder into the wood. "They didn't have us upload any native-language data. I only speak the star language."

With little effort, he allowed his body to mold into a form she would be more comfortable with. Flesh replaced the hard shell of his skin. His fangs retracted, as did his talons. When he'd finished the transformation only his golden eyes remained so that he could see her in the darkened forest.

"I am Lord Aleksej, Younger Duke of Draig," he said in the universal star language, trying to keep the eagerness from his voice. Like shifting and other secrets of his planet, the Draig did not share their language—not that anyone other than the locals wanted to learn it. "How did you come to be in the forest?"

"What are you, Lord Aleksej, Younger Duke of Draig?" she whispered, still pressing tight into the fallen tree.

"You make call me Alek. I am Draig, a dragon-shifter. Do not let my appearance before frighten you. I mean you no harm." He took a careful step

273

THE STUBBORN LORD

closer, lifting the crystal toward her. "I was meant to find you."

"Galaxy Brides sent you to track me," she said, as if knowing this to be a truth. "You can tell them you didn't find me. You can tell them I disappeared. I won't hurt anyone. I just want to go home. Please, you can understand that, can't you? I don't want to go to the ceremony. I just want to find a ride home. Please don't make me go back."

The woman wasn't dressed as a bride, but neither was he dressed fully like a groom. He didn't wear the mask. They shouldn't be talking, not like this. There were traditions. Though tradition allowed him to find a mate whenever the crystal glowed, he wasn't supposed to speak to her on the festival night until she made the symbolic gesture of choosing him.

"Please," she begged.

To find out more about Michelle's books visit www.MichellePillow.com

ABOUT MICHELLE M. PILLOW

New York Times & *USA TODAY* **Bestselling Author**

Michelle loves to travel and try new things, whether it's a paranormal investigation of an old Vaudeville Theatre or climbing Mayan temples in Belize. She believes life is an adventure fueled by copious amounts of coffee.

Newly relocated to the American South, Michelle is involved in various film and documentary projects with her talented director husband. She is mom to a fantastic artist. And she's managed by a dog and cat who make sure she's meeting her deadlines.

For the most part she can be found wearing pajama pants and working in her office. There may or may not be dancing. It's all part of the creative process.

Come say hello! Michelle loves talking with readers on social media!

www.MichellePillow.com

facebook.com/AuthorMichellePillow

twitter.com/michellepillow

instagram.com/michellempillow

bookbub.com/authors/michelle-m-pillow

goodreads.com/Michelle_Pillow

amazon.com/author/michellepillow

youtube.com/michellepillow

pinterest.com/michellepillow

COMPLIMENTARY EXCERPTS

HIS FROST MAIDEN

BY MICHELLE M. PILLOW

A Qurilixen World Novel

Space Lords Book 1

Empath and space pirate, Evan Cormier is obsessed with decoding an ominous premonition about his future. When a fellow crewman angered a spirit, the vengeful Zhang An took her wrath out on everyone in the vicinity. Evan just happened to be one of them. He's now facing a future in which he'll be forever alone.

Lady Josselyn of the House of Craven has been betrayed. With her home world on a Florencian moon under attack and her family dead, she finds herself at the mercy of the one who deceived them. There is only one thing left to do—die with honor.

But before she can join her family in the afterlife, she must first avenge all that she held dear. Falling in love with a pirate was never in the plan. Evan and his thieving crewmates might have delayed her fate, but they can't stop destiny.

His Frost Maiden Excerpt

Craven Estates, Earth Settlement, Florencia's Fifth Moon

"Lift her," the General ordered, his shiny boots walking away from her, taking her reflection with it.

Two men hauled her to her feet, holding her up by her arms. Josselyn suppressed a cry as they jerked her dislocated shoulder. She couldn't see their faces, didn't need to. Her body hurt so badly she couldn't tell where the pain was coming from anymore.

The one who'd betrayed them stood before her. General Jack Stephans. He'd deceived her family and the fifth moon settlement. He'd traded them in for money and power. Josselyn lifted her gaze briefly to the hard depths of the steel green eyes before her. She wanted to kick, to give one last good blow, to go down fighting, but she couldn't raise her limbs.

"Poor little Josselyn, so heartbreaking," the

HIS FROST MAIDEN

General grabbed her chin and swiped beneath her eye. He looked young, was in fact very young for his position, only a few years older than her six and twenty. And yet they all knew so much more of fighting than anyone their age should, than anyone ever should.

"We gave you a home," she whispered. "How could you do this? How could you join them?"

"You gave me a place in your stables," he spat, his grip tightening on her chin, bruisingly so. "Not a place at your table. Not a place by your side. Not equal. They gave me a rank, a title. They give me respect. They give me a place in this world."

"Jack," she said, her voice softening for the orphan boy they'd found over twenty years ago. If she begged him, maybe fate could be turned around; maybe this day could be erased. Fate had spit them out in a whirlwind of chance and deceit. Maybe all that had happened wasn't his fault. Maybe it wasn't hers. None of it mattered. None of it changed the fact that he had taken everything she held dear, everyone, and now he was robbing her of her family home. Her tone hardened and she closed her eyes. "General."

"Look at me, Josselyn," he said. His tone caught even as his grip on her face tightened until his fingers pressed the inside of her cheeks against her teeth. "You're so cold. Even now, your face is composed. Is one, lonely tear all the passion you can muster?"

"I am Lady Josselyn of the House of Craven." Her eyes opened slowly, focusing on the shiny white of his uniform. It gleamed with the orange glow coming from the fireplace. The material looked odd in the drabber earth tones many on the fifth moon wore. Theirs was a world based on Medieval Earth. Each moon in the Florencian system was different, each settlement patterned off a singular time in the human past, times that history had almost forgotten. But the principals of the ancestors who'd established the colonies no longer applied. Times were different now. What had started as preservation of history had turned into reality, into laws and a way of life they all believed in as generation after generation was raised into the worlds of the Florencian moons.

The General shook her by the face until finally she forced her eyes to meet his. He looked angry, hurt, wildly hopeful. "I can save you. I can say you had nothing to do with the treachery of your family. No one wants to kill a woman of noble blood. The line of Craven doesn't have to die. I will take your name; the name denied me by your father."

Was he serious? She knew he'd asked her father for her hand in marriage. In fact, she'd dismissed

HIS FROST MAIDEN

the proposal with the full knowledge he only asked because he wanted power. Did he think she could love him now? Want him? Take him into her bed?

He must have read the answer on her face because his own expression hardened. She knew Jack. He wouldn't ask again.

"I suppose not," he said, almost sad. "Even if you agreed, I could never trust you not to take a blade to my back. Not after today." He sighed heavily. "Not after this."

"Ago," she whispered, even her voice beginning to fail in its strength, "pugna quod int-"

"Quiet your tongue! This house is mine. Mine." He let go of her chin and her head drooped. "And you can die knowing that I have taken more than what you all refused to give me in life."

"A place at our table," Josselyn said, her tone softer still, the will to live leaving her. Her heart called out to her ancestors, to her dead family, begging them to come and get her.

"My table," he answered, stepping away. The General lifted a gun, pointing it at her head. She heard the telltale click of metal on metal. The weapon was not one found on the fifth moon. They fought with swords and axes, like the old medieval ways. Though technology was available, not using it was a point of honor. He must have brought the weapon from another moon. Perhaps the Victori-

283

ans? The Elizabethans? It appeared to be too old to be from much later in time.

"Do it, Jack." She didn't look at him as she waited for the final discharge of the gun, the loud bang before the end. When it didn't come, she repeated, the words a mere mouthing of her lips, "Do it."

"Speed you to a quick end, Josselyn Craven," Jack whispered. "You all brought this on yourselves."

To find out more about Michelle's books visit www.MichellePillow.com

LILITH ENRAPTURED

BY MICHELLE M. PILLOW

Divinity Warriors 1
Alternate Reality Romance

Sorin of Firewall lives in a land forever at war. In fact, the Starian men are so busy fighting, their marriage ceremony has been reduced to a "will of the gods" event where they simply pick a woman out of a lineup and claim her as a wife. With women becoming scarce, it's necessary to trade the offworld Divinity Corporation for brides. Duty-bound to attend the ceremony, he has no intention of picking a bride, let alone one from another dimension. Duty-bound to attend the ceremony, he has no intention of picking a bride, let alone one from another dimension. That is, until he sees

Lilith, the bewitching woman sent by the gods to reward—or punish?—him.

Lilith, a data analyst for Divinity, is betrayed by the Corporation and wakes up in a primitive, uncharted dimension filled with warriors who only know war and duty. But her initial fears of becoming a sex slave to a big beefy knight become all too real when a warrior of god-like proportions claims she's his new woman. As Lilith discovers, there are worse fates than being the focus of Sorin's skillful and earthy seduction.

First Chapter Excerpt

"The faster you make them come, the less time you must spend in their presence," Sera whispered, her words accented with an unfamiliar intonation. The tight fit of her white corset top squeezed her healthy waist and thrust up two very generous breasts. Long blue skirts billowed around her legs. She eyed the half dozen girls in the cell as she handed them loaves of bread. The need to be helpful shone from her sincere expression. "That is all they want—a vessel to find release in. Do not expect tenderness, but if you don't deny them, if you don't resist, you'll be treated fairly enough. And

LILITH ENRAPTURED

if you give them sons, you'll be greatly rewarded. Life here is not so bad."

Lilith Grian didn't move. She was still trying to get over the fact that she'd gone to bed in her own, lonely San LoFrancis apartment and awoke to find herself kidnapped and locked away in some small cell packed full of terrified women, with nothing but a long white robe over her body. The thick wool and shapeless design was a little to "sacrificial" for her tastes. A sniffle sounded next to her and Lilith glanced at the dark-haired woman crying next to her.

"This isn't happening, this isn't happening," the woman repeated, over and over. "Wake up, Edith, wake up."

Almost pleading, Sera shoved a loaf of bread toward Lilith. "I'm telling you how to best survive this place, please, listen. Spreading your thighs is an easy enough task for a decent life. Don't bring trouble upon yourself. Let them find release. They are not such boars when they get what they want."

Edith continued to rock herself, refusing bread and becoming more hysterical with every breath. Lilith wasn't sure who "they" were, but she sure as hell didn't like them already. Unlike Edith, she wasn't upset about the whole inter-dimensional travel scenario. As an historical and cultural analyst for the Divinity Corporation, it was her duty to jump from one plane of existence to another and collect intelligence on that world. She loved discovering the different intricate paths of the human experience, how one tiny event could change the course of humanity. What did concern Lilith was the fact that this jump wasn't assigned, and she was supposed to have two weeks off pending a board review of her last screwed-up mission.

Since Divinity had the only known source of top secret inter-dimensional travel technology on her plane, she guessed that maybe the review wasn't going her way. That or someone wanted her gone. Out of the four-hundred-thirty-six known dimensions, she didn't recognize this one as being charted, but to be fair it was difficult to determine much from inside a prison cell. As an analyst, Lilith had traveled to and studied most of the parallel planes. From what Sera described and the way everyone was dressed, this was new territory.

They shipped me off to an uncharted dimension?

Shock at her surroundings turned to outrage. This wasn't an accident. She would have had to have been drugged to be dressed in this outfit and sent through the portal unaware. Natural slips were extremely rare and completely predictable by the company. Sure as sunshine, a portal would not have opened up in her bedroom.

How dare they! One fuck-up that wasn't even my fault and I'm suddenly exiled?

She wondered how human this reality was. Some had vampires and werewolves, some had faeries and gnomes, and some had humanoids so alien her dimension's species were hardly compatible. Many of them had never even heard of dimensional travel or portals. Some societies were obsessed to the point of compulsion, some with power, some with medical advancement and some with gladiator fights to the death.

"I can't be here," Edith whispered, shaking her head as if to make it all go away.

Partly taking pity on the frightened woman and partly desperate to get her to shut up, Lilith asked, "Where are you from?"

"San Francisco," Edith said. "What's going on here? Who are these people? Is this a reality show?"

Lilith ran through possibilities in her mind, trying to narrow down the geography to the right plane. "Is that the United States or Dominative Republic?"

"United States," Edith mumbled, sniffing loudly.

Lilith nodded. No wonder the woman was scared. Her dimension had only theorized alternative realities. They weren't even close to learning how to control them. This would be like time travel to her.

"First, you're not crazy. This is another plane of existence you've stepped into." When the woman only looked confused, Lilith explained, "Looking at a foreign dimension is like looking at your world if it had evolved in a different way. To a point there are many similarities. Languages, generally, are relatively similar. Some people will look the same, but not be the same people. Certain events like natural disasters will be shared. Weather is the same and this is still Earth. These people are still human-ish."

Lilith frowned, studying the iron bars keeping them locked in. Apparently, this particular dimension hadn't made it too far past the Middle Ages— if the trencher to hold the bread, serving wench and barbaric mentality of "just make him come and keep him happy" was any indication.

"You're as crazy as they are," Edith declared, backing away from her.

So much for helping out my fellow humanoid.

The other women in the cell held themselves quiet. Each wore the white, shapeless dress with bare feet. A blonde woman whimpered pathetically, watching as a tall, black-haired woman paced in front of her as if she might pounce. The dark-

LILITH ENRAPTURED

skinned beauty strode with amazing grace and poise, much like a dancer or martial artist.

A redhead merely sat, staring at the bars as if she knew exactly what was happening and where she was. Her fingers picked absentmindedly at the long sleeve of her gown. She hadn't moved since they woke up that morning. The last prisoner, a well-endowed brunette, had pulled a thin metal clip out of her upswept hair and thrust it into the outside lock, trying to work the door free.

Suddenly, the brunette jerked her hand back and thrust the clip into her hair. A burly man dressed in a hard leather jerkin and dark breeches approached the cells, standing between the bars and the blue-grey stone wall on the other side of the narrow hall. Metal diamonds plated the leather, creating a symmetrical pattern over his thick chest. The guard crossed his thick arms, creating a veritable blockade more effective than the iron.

Lilith knew how to defend herself if the need arose, but he would be a hard opponent to beat. Well, to be honest, she hadn't actually practiced her defensive moves like she should have been according to Divinity employee policy. Her punches would only do so much damage and he had the muscle mass to absorb her blows with ease. A long, thin scar traced down the side of his cheek, adding a dangerous appeal to his look. Edith and the blonde whimpered. Lilith couldn't help but note that maybe she was the only one who thought the man appealing.

The warrior guard studied them one by one, not appearing pleased with what he saw. Then, motioning to the side, he beckoned another warrior man to appear next to him. "The flaxen one and the crying one. They do not carry themselves well. Take them and give them the philter."

Lilith automatically touched a lock of her straight, blonde hair. Her heart jumped a little in her chest, until she saw the guard look at the other flaxen-headed woman.

"What?" Edith screamed. "No, wait! I'll be good. I swear I'll be good. Please, don't hurt me. Please, I'll do anything you want. Do you want me to make you come? I will. I swear I will. I'll do you all!" To disprove her point, her body began to shake and she started bawling anew.

The guard looked disgusted by her display. Lilith couldn't say she blamed him. Where was the woman's honor? Her pride? If death was to come, there was nothing to be gained by tears. What she should be doing is analyzing their environment and calculating her escape.

The barred door opened and four men filed inside. Their massive warrior-like presence made her feel tiny in comparison as they crowded the cell. Two grabbed the now sobbing Edith and dragged her out. The blonde screamed, kicking and fighting as tears streamed down her face. The four remaining women held perfectly still. Lilith did not want to be grabbed next. The gods only knew what this "philter" was. It didn't sound pleasant.

As soon as the men were gone, the brunette went back to work, her face set as she tried to feel around the lock with her hairpin. The cell became eerily quiet now that the two women had been taken away.

"You won't be able to open it," the redhead said, staring at the lock picker. "Even if you did, there would be no escape. You'd have to fight through the warriors' hall, out of the guarded castle gates and run three strikes over open prairie until you reach the forest. Should you survive the wild beasts that live there, you'd soon find yourself prisoner to an even more vicious race of creatures —monsters so fierce and depraved they'll make you beg for death. Trust me, with the war going on in this forsaken place, we're in the better of the two sides."

"Who are you that we should trust what you say?" the brunette asked.

"Name's Paige," the redhead answered.

"Lilith," Lilith inserted, glad they'd finally started communicating. She didn't blame them for

LILITH ENRAPTURED

being cautious. All morning there had been a secret judging and assessing between them.

"What do they want with us?" The black-haired woman stopped pacing. All eyes turned to her. "Oh, I'm called Jayne."

"They want us to be their whores," Paige answered, bitterness seeping into her hard tone. "They don't call it that, but that's what they want— a subservient woman to rub their feet and spread her legs. If you don't, they get pissed and the whole lot of them stares at you like you are demon spawn incarnate and blames you for your chosen warrior's bad mood. It's either fuck them and suck them, or you're treated like the bottom rung of Starian society."

"Again, I ask, why should we trust you? We don't know you." The brunette continued to try to pick the lock. "You could be a plant sent here to make us behave with horror stories of what's beyond the tree line."

"I don't care if you trust me, but I know what I'm talking about. This isn't my first time in a cage." Paige tilted her head back and sighed. "They'll be coming to get us soon."

"What's your name, locksmith?" Jayne asked the brunette.

"Karre."

"Well, Karre," Jayne said, "I don't think we

have much of a choice. If we all work together, maybe we stand a chance. Now, I don't know how we all got here and at this point I don't think it matters, but I do know I'm not staying to spend the rest of my life as some guy's sex toy."

"I agree." Lilith stood, hoping Jayne would have a logical solution they could use. "We need a plan."

"Fine," Karre grumbled.

Paige opened her eyes and shook her head. "Don't look to me to join your little band. You're only fooling yourselves. I've been to the Hanging Forest. I made it all the way to the Starian borders and I've seen the creatures that wait beyond."

"What about a dimension jump?" Lilith asked. "Does anyone know if this place has inter-dimensional travel technology?"

"A what?" Paige furrowed her brow in confusion.

"Staria? It's too primitive. They don't have the technology here," Karre said. "I got a glimpse of the castle when they brought me to this cell. Through a door I saw servants cart water from a well in buckets and the drive wasn't paved. No artificial lights or motorized vehicles. Though there were several large horses."

"I've never been here," Jayne contributed, "but

LILITH ENRAPTURED

I'm inclined to agree from what I've observed. These prisons don't use lasers or shocks."

"Someone's coming." Karre pulled her arms out from between the bars. She thrust her lockpicking tool back into her upswept hair.

A new guard arrived, dressed similar to the other men she'd seen. His nose had a crook across the bridge. He frowned. "Only three new ones?"

"It's all they sent us," said the man who'd ordered the other two women away.

"How's it going, Edward?" Paige taunted, her face hardening to hide all emotion. "I see the nose is healing nicely."

"Lady Paige," Edward growled, glaring at her as if he wanted to pull the sword from his waist and run her through.

"Open the door, Eddie," Paige taunted. "Let me break it again."

Edward grumbled, but didn't answer.

"I thought there were five new," another of Edward's fellow barbarians said, completely ignoring Paige.

"What's wrong, Brock? Don't I count anymore in your little ledger?" Paige taunted. Lilith kept quiet, observing as was her nature to do.

"You are not new," Brock stated, frowning at her in disapproval. "Your lord is waiting for you and I do hope his punishment is harsh."

Paige's smirk faltered. Brock grinned victoriously.

"You already have one of these guys?" Karre whispered, grabbing Paige's arm.

"Two were not suitable. They were taken away," Edward said, answering his companion. His nostrils flared in distaste. "Too weak."

"Three will have to do," Brock answered, sighing. As the two men walked off, he added, "I'll tell my Sera to make ready."

A long silence filled the cell, broken only when Paige whispered, "Ladies, welcome to Battlewar Castle."

If Lord Sorin hated anything, he hated waste—wasted resources, wasted hours, wasted lives. And, as far as he was concerned, these breeding ceremonies were a waste of time. Nothing in the process of prancing women before the warriors, who then picked them based on an urge, guaranteed a well-made match. Their ancestors had the right idea when they'd raided villages and took the women they wanted. At least the raids served three purposes—the need for men to find a woman to put into their bed, the need for men to have sons and the need for men to fight their wars. Besides, going on a raid would not take the warriors away from the battlefront, not like traveling back to Battlewar Castle in the northernmost part of their kingdom for a breeding ceremony.

Women were scarce in this hard land. Sons became a necessity and their natural evolution seemed to answer the call with more sons than daughters—when they did have children. Their low birthrate wasn't from lack of trying when the warriors were home, but war took them away all too often. Sometimes forever.

Sorin glanced around his castle chambers, the place he always stayed when he came to Battlewar. Ever since his own castle, Firewall, burned to the ground, this was as close to a stationary home as he had. Like all male rooms, the decorations were sparse—a large bed with a mammoth-wolf fur coverlet, a large wall filled with every weapon he'd ever owned in chronological order, a fireplace, comfortable chair, a trunk for his personal belongings and two doors.

The black stone walls pressed in on him. He shouldn't be here. He should be at the encampment with the other men. What did he care if tradition dictated he at least attempt to take a breeding partner, a mate, a bride, a whatever the women liked to call the joining nowadays. He had a bride once and it did him little good. Bianka, the accursed wench, was dead and it suited him just fine not to replace her.

Still moist from his recent bath, he adjusted his hips on the chair and wrapped his callused fingers around the semi-erect member between his thighs. Granted, self-satisfaction wasn't as gratifying as the real thing, but it would keep his head level during the ceremony. He would never forgive himself if he did something stupid. The longer his kind went without the exhausting pleasure of the bed, the more their moods were said to be altered. Sorin grunted. He thought he did just fine without a woman.

He gripped his cock hard, squeezing in irritation as he tried not to think of how he wanted to be far away from there. It didn't take long for his erection to reach full capacity and begin to ache. Veins strained along the firm flesh, leading a familiar trail over his shaft from thick base to smooth tip. The water dried and the rough texture of his war-hardened hand caused an insistent friction along his shaft. Nothing about the grip reminded him of the soft folds of a woman and that's the way he liked it —hard and empty.

He stroked fast and tight. The muscles in his stomach tightened. His body knew its part and didn't need to be romanced into climaxing. Closing his eyes, he let the end come. Physical release sated one hunger, the feast being prepared below stairs would take care of the other. By morn, he'd ride out with his brother to join the battlefront.

Sorin stood and stretched his hands over his head. The low fire had dried the water from his naked flesh. All this sitting around and reflecting didn't sit well on his mind. Completely comfortable in his nakedness, he strode to the trunk and flung it open. Tradition demanded he dress nicely this evening, even though he much preferred armor to silken threads.

But hate all this nonsense as he may, it was his turn to sit before the stage and watch the newest batch of women being paraded before them. And, like the several times before, he'd do nothing but sit and wait and curse the hours of his life that were being wasted.

For a complete, up-to-date booklist, visit www. MichellePillow.com

PLEASE LEAVE A REVIEW

THANK YOU FOR READING!

Please take a moment to share your thoughts by leaving a review.

Be sure to check out Michelle's other titles at www.michellepillow.com

Printed in Great Britain
by Amazon